The 50-Word Stories of 2022 Microfiction for Lovers or Quick Reads 50 Give or Take #2 by Vine Leaves Press

The 50-Word Stories of 2022
Compiled and edited by Jessica Bell and Elaina Battista-Parsons
Copyright © 2022 Vine Leaves Press
All rights reserved.

Print Edition
ISBN: 978-618-86077-5-0
Published by Vine Leaves Press in Greece 2022

Cover design by Jessica Bell
Interior design by Amie McCracken

A catalogue record of this work is available from The National Library of Greece

Hand

He asked for my hand! Even more incredulous was that my father agreed. Father was not the kind of man to believe him, but he agreed. Hesitantly, I held out my hand. "Any chance of foreign travel?" asked my dad, as the palm reader squinted at my fate lines.

Ayushya is a mechanical engineer who loves mathematics, the language of symbols, and loves language, the instrument of liberation. Medium *@ayushyasukhiye*

We Got Your Backup

She was eight and it was her first time singing at the Karaoke Bar. On the first line of her song, "Barbie Girl" she froze, intimidated by the garish crowd. Her mother, her many aunts, and her sisters jumped up on the stage and sang until she thawed. A Standing O.

Michael Walker is a writer living and working in Newark, Ohio, and on the Earth.

Little Things

Tall green plants wait in the greenhouse with that distinctive fresh tomato smell, intensified in the humidity. A small girl holds her grandfather's hand. They've nurtured these plants together. Her reward: plucking the first ripe one, eating it, apple style, as he looks on, overwhelmed with love.

Karen Al-Ghabban is a lover of words and languages, and she is married with two children and two dogs.

Eight Syllables

The bed is still unmade and the indent warm where you lay last night and lied, *There's no one else but you.* Despite your hollow words, I've crafted mine: *Gone for a ride, may not be back.* Eight syllables slouch against an empty glass without an excuse or backward glance.

Since the only poem she wrote in high school was red-penciled "extremely maudlin," Carolyn Martin is amazed she has continued to write. *carolynmartinpoet.com*

Selfie

An idyllic day, perfect for three teenage girls posing for a selfie on the tracks. A gentle breeze and chirping birds mask the sound of a freight train fast approaching. The camera clicks as horror stamps the moment on the engineer's eye. Bliss will never look or feel the same.

Marc Littman, a former journalist, writes flash fiction, novels, and plays.

Suspension

Through the tangles of hair thrashing her face, she glimpses something yellow in her periphery and turns toward it: a handmade sign taped to the pylon. Need help?

A phone number. Fingers stir inside her pocket, seeking her phone.

The bridge will still be here later if she needs it.

Elizabeth Barton is a writer/editor living in Chicago with her husband, two cats, and more than a little self-doubt. *lizardesque.wordpress*

The Old Maid

O'er near the sandy beaches, an old maid was found to tell. Tell she did, so profoundly, that o'ers sought to hear her words. "Come and listen" she said *proudly*. Her words set to rise, ears we lent as she then proudly began to chant, "Come to me."

Katrenia Busch is an author, film critic, journal reviewer, and published poet. LinkedIn *@katreniabusch*

Roam and Rest

In the midst of chasing dreams and luck, I got lost. Clinging to everything exciting led me nowhere specific. They said, "Zeal and power drive the pace, keep you moving." I asked, "If all I did, from the start, was run and wander, don't I at least deserve a rest?"

Shreesham Pandey is a teenage author, writer, poet and much more, who dabbles in everything that he finds creative, wild, and optimistic. *shreeshampandey.blogspot*

Two Final Things

As the ex-astronaut slipped into a coma, he remembered two final things: how the earth had looked rising up over the Sea of Storms and that his landlady had cautioned him to always put a bathmat down when showering in the old porcelain tub.

Michael S. Walker is a writer living and working in Newark, Ohio. Facebook *@michaels.walker*

Blink

We pulled behind the line of cars stopped at the intersection. The traffic light blinked green. No one moved. Our irate driver yelled. "Moron, get off your phone." Horns blared. The car ahead of us jerked forward. The light blinked red. The noise of crunching metal reverberated through the streets.

Catherine Shields is a retired teacher who resides in Miami, Florida where she writes about parenting, disabilities, and self-discovery.

Addicted

His lips parched as he gazed at her slender neck. The elegant way she sat on his table created a pit in his stomach. Her body glowed. It pained him to not reach out to her. He salivated as he stroked the label, and whispered her name, *Merlot*.

Ayushya is a mechanical engineer who loves mathematics, the language of symbols, and loves language, the instrument of liberation. Medium *@ayushyasukhiye*

Grandma

Twelve and I raced to get there. I was met with the smell of rising bread: yeast and the promise of peanut butter banana sandwiches and then the radio. Grandma made the best bread; and in the afternoon she taught me how to paint and imagine myself in a new way.

Michael Yoder is a writer living in Victoria, B.C. Canada.

What She Knows

We never speak, but she knows loads about me. That I like bourbon whiskey. And betting on the horses. That I had a lover whose letters I no longer care to keep.

She watches silently from her post near the open, garbage bins—the Madame DeFarge of the town dump.

Jan Bartelli is a former journalist, a more-or-less retired attorney, and a less-is-more writer of creative nonfiction.

I Had That Dream Again Last Night

We were buying milk at that 7-11 when a robber shot me right in the mouth. I couldn't speak or cry out, but ribbons of giant text gushed out of me until I deflated completely. Blood, milk, unread words everywhere, and then that kid started telling a joke. You laughed.

Robb Lanum is a failed screenwriter in Los Angeles who has fallen in love with the short form.

Death Trains

Chimps living in captivity are known to defiantly throw their turds at their keepers, and so as he looks out on the railyard, where special police in black uniforms enforce the loading of a line of boxcars, the inoffensive little clerk with the clipboard is glad people aren't like chimps.

Howie Good is the author most recently of the poetry collection *Gunmetal Sky* with Thirty West Publishing.

Lilian Said

'Safety? There is no such place.' Our labored syllables pick up. Between land lines the narratives of our worlds meet. Sticks rattle, an end game runs. Nuanced participles define the out of tune, hope, hoping, less. Somewhere in the frozen south they cry in the morning.

Jenny Dunbar continues to make ceramics and haikus in these strange times.

Taking Inventory

No earthquakes today or brush fires. Fireplace cricket didn't keep me up. Bread on the counter still fresh. No friend called with a cancer diagnosis. Kids got home after partying. Mom feels good, laughed with friends. Guess I'll get off the couch, stretch the tightness from my back.

Phyllis Schwartz is a former journalist living in a dreamy California beach town trying to color outside the lines, the headlines.

Apple Butter

Granddaddy grew an apple orchard above the frost line on Shewbird Mountain. A hard freeze nipped the goldenrods and mums, but the trees burned with brushstrokes of autumn. Winesaps thumped on the forest. We diced fruit and made apple butter in an old black pot over a fire.

Brenda Kay Ledford is a member of North Carolina Writer's Network. She's received the Paul Green Award a dozen times for her work. *blueridgepoet.blogspot*

King?

Was the proud owner of a king-sized bed when I was single.

Lost 95% of ownership after I got engaged.

Looking forward to my Marriage.

Divya George is an occasional blogger. *offbeatscribbles.wordpress*

Arrival

Having just arrived, they looked exhausted. But the dunes, house, and beach faded the packing, traffic, and screaming.

"Our groceries are here," she observed, seeing stacked bags on the sand.

"Why didn't they take them up?"

The landlady appeared, feet bare, swimsuit dripping.

"You're here next week!" she yelled.

Emmy-award-winner Amy Bass is a writer, professor, and sport thinker. *amybass.net*

Pricked Out for Pleasure

Heads bowed, they sat, bashful, coy, on their wedding thrones as around them the noisy, colorful, throng celebrated. Complicit, a phial of blood made them laugh behind closed doors. They had recognized each other's desires at first sight, and friendship solid, the deception was complete. That's why they had both worn lavender.

Karen Al-Ghabban is a lover of words and languages, and she is married with two children and two dogs.

Pink Hat

She put on her pink hat, spread hummus on the crispbread, and decided it would taste better on a snowy cliff, just not here. Wherever here was. She couldn't remember the last time she didn't feel lost. She stepped outside, and the neighbor whispered, "Shirley, where are your clothes?"

Adrian Voss lives in Colorado and enjoys the weather while exploring the silence and experimenting with genre. *adrianvoss.com*

The Visit

An exuberant six-year-old scrambles into bed, prepared for the tooth fairy's arrival. A polished silver eggcup cradles the refreshment of honey water, the window ajar to allow safe flight inside. Dawn: gold glitter transverses from the child's head to the window. The cup is empty: a silver dollar awaits discovery.

Deb Obermanns is an avid traveler, lover of storytelling, and international school teacher.

Education

In the smoking rubble everyone split up, with nothing between us and history but bleach and needles. Everyone forgot but me. I studied things made of spells and wheels. It was a fury, and we were all in it, but I didn't forget. Then, at the office, you said something.

Gregg Williard is a writer and artist based in Madison, Wisconsin.

Behind Her House

Forest-muffled shots behind her house. My husband, armed and dangerous, bounced headlights down the easement with me on his shirt-pocket phone. Emerging from the trees, the thirty-something was still a kid: alcohol on his breath, meth behind his eyes, hand behind his back. But who fired next?

MaxieJane Frazier is a western writer, a military veteran, and an editor with Birch Bark Editing. *maxiejanefrazier.com*

Blame it on Guapo

One morning, a puppy named Guapo found a root to pull. Nothing happened. He pulled again. Harder. China moved closer to Spain. New York flew into Wisconsin. Young women crashed into old men, confusing some, delighting others. Birds began to bark. Snakes started singing. That's why we have climate change.

K. T. Maclay is an occasional writer living in the cultural center of Oaxaca de Juarez, Mexico.

Blessed Be

Like the dutiful daughter they think she is, she's packed and headed for home within thirty minutes of picking up her mama's phone call … *it won't be long now* … her mama gets out between sobs. She's going home. Not to mourn, but to rejoice. It's over. It's finally over.

Alana King is in the final stages of her PhD. She hopes to be done soon. *alanacking.com*

Birthday Party

Balloons lolled drunkenly on red leashes. Their helium had leaked, and their skin was loose and wrinkled. Danny squeezed the sad, sagging cases to slip in a needle. The essence of each balloon slipped out with a sigh. At least they wouldn't have to go through this again.

Ricky Monahan Brown is the author of the survival memoir, *Stroke: A 5% chance of survival*, one of The Scotsman's Scottish Books of 2019. Facebook *@rickymonahanbrown*

Later

Meditation and Positive Affirmations are the keys to my success. It's also important to visualize getting exactly what you want. I practice these things daily while emptying the bathroom waste can, carefully collecting your hair and nail clippings. Later I'll manifest just the right spell to change my future.

Emily Kupinsky is an Artist, Writer, and Maker of Things. Instagram *@emmysez*

Frugality

"Great haul at the Dollar Store today, Honey ..."

"Whatdja get?"

"A can-opener and a lead paperweight."

"Another can-opener? The last six didn't work."

"But they're only a dollar!"

"What was all that bangin' I heard comin' from the kitchen?"

"Makin' lunch."

"Why are you splattered in Spaghettios?"

Clyde Always is an accomplished cartoonist, poet, painter, novelist, and Vaudevillian entertainer. *clydealways.com*

Screenings

The movies start playing deep inside my head well before the lights dim. There's never an intermission and they continue for long minutes even after the credits roll. As the final frames flicker and fade to black, I see the weary projectionist is already slouched on the bus heading home.

Walt Thomas, author of *Smokehouse Stomp*, co-hosts the Charbroiled Chats podcast.

Peace

I spot her as I get off the elevator. Leaning against a post at Nordstrom's, she checks her phone. She hasn't changed – still stocky, in jeans, a shaggy pullover, and clunky shoes. She has agreed to meet, make a tentative peace, and become a daughter again.

Evie Groch is an educator who has fallen into the addictive habit of writing.

Exuberance

On the zebra crossing, a boy, bucket and spade in hand, is hurried across by Mum, baby sister in tow. He halts, excitedly, and raises his hand police style, to stop me. Mum grimaces. I laugh, and salute back. The little boy giggles with delight and blows me a kiss.

Karen Al-Ghabban is a lover of words and languages, and she is married with two children and two dogs.

The Tree

What is so lovely as a tree? Nine and three quarter acres of them in Washington Square Park. An older man carefully chooses a big one, stands and holds his hands flat on it for two minutes. Head bowed. Listening to the heartwood? Praying to Gaia? He sidles away, smiling.

Lou Giansante writes, records sound, and tries to put them together.

The Laundry

Frederick threw another shovelful of laundry, industrial drums echoing. A slight movement caught his eye and he spun, unwashed cloth looming. A balled-up sock tumbled. He breathed out, reaching for more work. Yet as he rose, there, scurrying between equipment, a pile of laundry scuttled. Frederick pounded after it.

Rachel Lentz lives all around Eastern Washington and graduated with a bachelors in creative writing from Washington State University. *rachellentz.wixsite.com*

The Queen of Kennington

We met on a bus on Kennington Road. She seemed confused so I offered to help. We walked for a bit then sat on a bench. She sighed. She said she used to be a Queen Elizabeth look-alike, then waved regally to each bus passing by.

Ellen Fox is an award-winning theatre playwright, who has also written for radio, film, and television.

Making Lunch

Jack Kerouac suggested the title *Naked Lunch* for William S. Burroughs' novel. Allen Ginsberg, who was editing the book with Kerouac, asked what the title meant. Kerouac said they would figure it out later. And Burroughs? He was in the kitchen slapping lettuce and tomato on reality sandwiches.

Howie Good is the author of the prose poetry collection *Famous Long Ago*, forthcoming from Laughing Ronin Press.

Scrub Oak and White Cedar

The smell of low tide in a brackish back-creek creeps into my memory. I am barefoot and running down a dirt path lined with scrub oak and white cedar. I struggle to catch up to my father, guided by the sound of his voice, "Come on now, don't be dawdling."

Barbara Elliott is a Philadelphia-based artist, writer, and lover of baseball.

Out

Sunday, the gap between. Houses flex, releasing forgotten corners where afterthoughts wait to be collected. Light breaks through net edges, inside closed rooms. Safer to breathe quietly through these fragile spaces. She carries her backpack downstairs, creeps across the hall, front door ajar, the skin of her tooth stinging.

Jenny writes every day and makes abstract ceramics.

A Rose in the Cemetery

A life etched in stone and broken relationships, perhaps. A Rose in the cemetery curled up in the grass, sleeps in the sunshine safely within the churchyard walls of brick and wrought iron. Forever devoted to the ones that await beneath. You are such a good dog, they tell her.

Patricia Pollack is a nurse educator and writer, ready to jump in the car for the next adventure. Yahoo *@patriciajpollack*

Dive Partner

Beneath the water's surface is our mindfulness hour. Preparing to dive, shouts offshore alarm us! Eerily, from the morning fog, 101 Haitian refugees cling to a makeshift boat adrift. Some swim euphorically toward us, tears falling from their hollow faces. Shouts of "Miami" echo. We sob back, "No, Cuba!"

Deb Obermanns is an avid traveler, lover of storytelling, and international school teacher.

Match Over

He watched anxiously, beads of sweat dripping from his temples. The ball flew in as the final whistle blew. The crowd roared. All he could see was the drink toss over as she jumped in joy on the big screen.

Radhika Baruah is a bookworm experimenting with wordplay. *beingmeema. wordpress.com*

Full Moon

A spotted, white orb gleamed through the thick fog on an Autumn evening in San Francisco. Two Midwestern tourists, out for a charming stroll, found themselves perturbed by its eerie glow. An eccentric local, impoverished, and beltless, slept face down on a piece of cardboard, apparently unaware of his condition.

Clyde Always is an accomplished cartoonist, poet, painter, novelist, and Vaudevillian entertainer. *clydealways.com*

Young Shoppers in Love

She pinballs through the racks of clothes and it's hard for him to keep his arm locked around her. You can actually see his muscles tightening, loosening, then tightening again as she moves. She can take him for granted if she wants to, but he will never let her go.

Greg Bowers lives near York, PA.

The Robins

The first beat itself to death on its cage bars. We had left it at day camp while we vacationed. The second died when Mother took nail scissors to amputate a broken leg. I'll never forget its screams. But ah, the third. It fledged, came back to visit the next summer. Hopped up on the stoop and cocked its head. Sweet.

Hannah Poole loves retirement in the city but misses the country of her childhood.

I Love You

At the carnival, he handed her a bear prize holding a heart that read, "I love you," like a billboard. They were just friends. Weren't they? She panicked. "I don't like stuffed animals with messages on them." She ripped the heart from its paws.

A special education teacher by day, Theresa Milstein writes middle grade, YA, and dabbles in poetry. *theresamilstein.blogspot.com*

Yes!

"No." He pulls back a little hand from the power outlet.

"No." He stops scattering cereal over the floor.

"No." He freezes mid-lunge toward the neighbor's skittish dog.

"All I ever say is no," I think, deflating.

Then, "Do you love me, Mommy?" he asks, arms outstretched.

"Yes!" I say.

Melissa Miles is a children's book author, certified educator, registered nurse, and board chair of Superhero Success Foundation, Inc. Twitter *@melissajmiles*

Timeless

Strangers, they sat side by side on the bus heading into town.

He said, "Excuse me, do you know the time?" She looked at her watch, offered a broad smile and replied, "Yes." Then turned away.

"Oh," he said, not quite knowing what to do with that information.

Ellen Fox is an award-winning theatre playwright, who has also written for radio, film, and television.

More That Unites Us ...

Two women, one niqabed, one sleeveless, queueing. "I haven't got all day," snaps Niqab. In that moment, sleeveless has all her remaining perceptions erased, and turns, converses, united in frustration. The impolite question escapes her lips unintentionally: "Why?" Eyes smiling, amused, Niqab replies, "Have you got all day?"

Karen Al-Ghabban is a lover of words and languages, and she is married with two children and two dogs.

Spiderlings

A speck crawls up the wall, then dozens, then hundreds, emerging from their sacs. Body rigid, save my eyes darting from walls, to ceiling, to nightstand. Wriggling itches cross my skin; climb my arm. Panic as little legs tickle my nose and lips. I hold my breath … until I can't.

D.J. Kozlowski writes to escape. Facebook @djwrites

Mama's Pearls

Chipped and yellowed from years of wear, I would often see her finger them, lovingly.

Her eyes glazed and distant. They just appeared one day, around her neck.

She didn't say; I didn't ask. Papa never noticed them. She's gone now—buried in her favorite blue dress, and faded pearls.

R. S. Raniere writes short stories, poetry, and Christian nonfiction, and will have a first novel published. roseanns-ramblings.com

Garibaldi

Garibaldi stands tall in Washington Square, hand on sword, ready to lead.

Pasquale stops by each morning, salutes, and pledges allegiance.

"Io ti saluto!"

A boy with a skateboard and green hair takes a puff and stares.

Lou Giansante writes, records sounds, and tries to put them together.

Man on a Mission

He wasn't a big man, but he had the fire of God when he railed against the company sharks. Later I learned he was lynched in Butte. Found him hanging from a trestle, a note pinned to his leg, "First and last warning." Those mining companies didn't take kindly to union organizers.

Barbara Elliott is a Philadelphia-based artist, writer, and lover of baseball.

59¢

Thirteen minutes left and even the towels are dry. I hate wasting 59¢, offer my leftover time to the woman three driers down. She takes her eyes off her whirling clothes. "Thanks, dear, I got enough on this one. Double blessing! It's a double blessing!" Her grin saves my morning.

Joan Larkin likes reading in the sun outside a New Jersey laundromat. *joanlarkin.com*

Not About Dad

"It isn't about the car, it's about Dad," he lied.

"Oh, now you're some big fan of Dad?"

He makes a sharp right turn.

"You only want the car 'cause it's cool."

He shrugs, "It is a cool car."

The car then makes a gurgling noise and cuts off.

Yuki Silva is a graduate of Stockton University, with a literature degree, excited to join the writing world.

Fire

"Don't worry," he heard the girl say to her friend as their ball tangled in the power lines overhead. "Those are our Jewish neighbors."

He stood and closed the window.

"The firemen said to air out as long as possible," she protested.

He shook his head, hoping she didn't hear.

Emmy-award-winner Amy Bass is a writer, professor, and sport thinker. *amybass.net*

Reality Check

If you're ever feeling especially cute, if your stylist gave you just the right haircut, if you feel perky, and your tail is all bushy and you're ready to go out and have fun," he said, "My suggestion is to run right down and get a passport picture taken."

K. T. Maclay is an occasional writer living in the cultural center of Oaxaca de Juarez, Mexico.

Ontogeny

Last year, she'd imagined placing herself inside a paper bag with a banana. Just the way it turned mangos tender and fragrant, it would spur her development. She'd catch up with the other girls. Now under continual assault by leering eyes, she wished for that paper bag to hide inside.

Elizabeth Barton is a writer/editor living in Chicago with her husband, two cats, and more than a little self-doubt. *lizardesque.wordpress.com*

Gobsmacked

A man of words. With a pristine paperback by a literary genius secured in his pocket, students are mesmerized as he recites poetry or describes the attributes of a vignette. Then two gametes meet—a simple start. A newborn girl! His eyes beam with joy and he is rendered speechless.

Deb Obermanns is an avid traveler, lover of storytelling, and international school teacher.

Just Say Yes

A classical concert played near their secluded spot on a bench in the park. Every part of her tingled from the violins to the warm breeze to the boy next to her. She waited for him to fumble his way through his feelings for her, so she could finally say yes.

A special education teacher by day, Theresa Milstein writes middle grade, YA, and dabbles in poetry. *theresamilstein.blogspot.com*

Never Gave Her a Hand Again

Mary Contrary played "She loves me, she loves me not," with the fingers of my right hand. One twist, they loosened. Second twist, out they came. Ow! Ow! Ow! Ow! Ow!

It ended in, "she loves me," but I said I had my doubts. Foolishly, I let her try again.

Michael Drezin is a lawyer and a storyteller, or the other way around.

Germany (Dachau)

My parents are arguing about me.

Mom says, "She's only twelve. It could scar her for life."

Dad asks, "But what about the invaluable lesson?"

I see lamp shades made of human skin, thousands of dead children's shoes. I thought ovens were only for baking yummy apple pie.

Ellen Sollinger Walker is a retired classical pianist and psychologist living the good life in Florida.

The Meaning of Things

A young woman stops in a faded photograph, half-smiling on a black-and-white staircase, feeling beautiful in her black-and-white dress. But there are candles in her eyes. Is it her birthday, or is she looking at someone she loves?

Greg Bowers lives near York, Pennsylvania.

You Just Don't Know Yet

Another box flew across the floor and landed at Go-Go's feet. A woman, the source of the flying boxes, followed through the doorway.

"Who are you?" she demanded.

"No one."

"Course y'are", came the quick response. "You just don't know it yet."

Finally thought Go-Go, smiling. "Someone who sees me."

Gail Byrd is an actor, a book reviewer, and a vocational specialist who enjoyed zoom acting during the pandemic. *gailbyrd.com*

Unexpected

Why do they scream so loudly? he thought. The door had been unlocked—an invitation. Its oiled hinges were silent as he closed it behind him. Shoes off, he made no sound as he crept upstairs. "I'm home!" he shouted. The excitement of his daughters nearly blew out his eardrums.

Alison McBain is an award-winning author, editor, and scribbler of comics about motherhood. Medium *@amcbain*

Time

The machete-wielding man's grey eyes glazed as he muttered, "The time is now."

Emily showed no fear.

"Such a silly expression," she said. "Have you ever wondered about it?" His confusion evident, he lowered his arm. Enough time for Emily to pull a pistol from her purse and shoot.

Apple Gidley, currently living in the Caribbean, is a global nomad who writes historical fiction, essays, and more. *applegidley.com*

Algorithmed Out

Cities planned by algorithms are more just, Oliver believed, balancing priorities to benefit more and inconvenience fewer. He'd written good code, used clean data, understood bias elimination. The municipality's letter was crisp and to the point. "Your building will be demolished on 02/12/2021. Consult the city portal for alternative accommodation."

Judy Backhouse writes future fiction as an imaginative escape from research into technology and society. *judybackhouse.com*

Centrifugal Force

Unpolished fingernails nearly pierce the worn Naugahyde rim as she plummets toward the ground. Jolted left then right, she confidently faces the next roller coaster thrill. Fighting centrifugal force, she looks into the mirror and knows she'll be okay. She's quite familiar with rugs being pulled from under her feet.

Shauna Lee McCarty enjoys writing and the daily belly laughter provided by her husband.

False Accusations

She never cursed that poppet. Or cast any spells. The blighted crops and early frost weren't her doing. But the town needed a scapegoat, and I needed to regain my husband's affections. As the flames climbed past the ropes binding her, the screams drowned the guilty pounding of my heart.

Melissa Miles is a children's book author, certified educator, registered nurse, and board chair of Superhero Success Foundation, Inc. Twitter @melissajmiles

Ocean Memories

The colors paraded in the sky as the sun descended into its ocean bed. Warm light blanketed the deck, clinging to it in desperation as the dark tendrils of night battled their way to supremacy. Memories of happier times exploded upon the horizon; before the embrace of darkness smothered them.

Damien is passionate about writing and reimagining the lost era of pulp fiction. His work centers on the creepy and the macabre.

Healing

He faced the computer with disgust, his fingers white and shaking. Someone said writing would help his healing faster than the insulin injection and pink drugs in his drawer. Five hours later, a blank page stared back at him.

Martin Chrispine Juwa is a Malawian writer who enjoys spending time with strangers.

When The Crows Came for Me

Straight up, a single crow cawed repeatedly atop the highest branch of my oldest tree, pausing between cries as though listening, its silences consistently paced. Suddenly the bird was soaring downward, behind it another crow, following the plunge, then a dozen more, cawing in pursuit, darkening the sky, overshadowing everything.

Bob Thurber is the author of 6 books. Over the years his work has received a long list of awards and been included in over sixty anthologies. *bobthurber.net*

Sounds

Coffee perking, slurping tea, voices bitch in unison. Machines beep, the arm of a paper cutter squeaks, guitar strings tune. Keyboards click, desk drawers slam and a strident bell commands attention. Front doors fling open, and heels quicken down the hall. "Good morning beautiful children!"

Deb Obermanns is an avid traveler, lover of storytelling, and international school teacher.

Love

My grandson finished opening his gifts on Christmas morning.
Wrapping paper hung everywhere like a Salvador Dahli
painting. Suddenly my grandson said, "You didn't get any pres-
ents!" Running to his room, he returned with a gift bag for me.
Inside was his most treasured hot wheels car.

Ami Offenbacher-Ferris lives in Wilmington, NC and writes poetry, flash fiction,
fiction and creative nonfiction. Vocal Media *@gypsie-ami-offenbacher-ferris*

How Was Your Day?

All I hear are low notes and misery. Tell me instead of boats, clouds,
sex, and bad ideas. Be impersonal. Shocking. Off-kilter. Abduct me
with a dangerous tale. Tell me you like the way I hold my drink.
Whisper something stirring. Make me nervous. Be my stranger.
Just for tonight.

Pasquale Trozzolo is a retired madman from Kansas, USA who continues to complicate
his life by living out as many retirement clichés as possible. Facebook *@poetpasquale*

Heavendrome

He had adapted his airfield into an assisted-suicide business. Climate and plagues had changed everything. Most customers chose to hook their nooses to weather balloons and leave this world drifting into the sky. But loved ones objected, and they were coming. Every night, he duct-taped his revolver to his hand.

Rusty Allen is author of the debut novel *Ella's War* (Vine Leaves Press 2023), and he is a career freelance writer and owner of The Writers Studio. *writersstudio.com*

Lace Dreams

The lace tablecloth lifted gently in the breeze, then settled down, as though finally resigned to giving up dreams of living out its existence as a veil or dress. A stain, brown now, but originally red, in the far corner. Ketchup. Another in the center. Yellowish-brown. Tea. Probably.

Susi Lovell is a short story writer living in Montreal. *susilovell.com*

Sled Dog Couch Dreams

Nila patrols a dog yard with two dozen kaleidoscoped husky eyes. "Eat!" she barks, "temperatures'll drop to thirty below tonight!" She watches her friends lick their bowls clean and enter a straw-stuffed barn under the Aurora. Nila nests next to a wood-stuffed stove, and dreams.

Todd K. Denick is a writer, educator, and former Alaskan living in Germany with his wife, son, and two dogs. Facebook *@todd-k-denick*

Speed Date

There are two parts in every relationship. In the first part, we learn everything we hate about the other person. In the second, we learn everything we hate about ourselves. Lucky for us, she says, we've only just met.

Pedro Ponce is the author of *The Devil and the Dairy Princess: Stories*. Twitter @ *pedroeponce*

Nothing Matters

Although I'd seen nothing, my husband's infatuation with Emma tormented me. Their fingers almost brushing? Nothing. Their overheard laughter? More nothing. I kept watching them. Then, one night, all through a long dinner party, they never spoke to each other, only to other people. I'd seen enough of their nothing.

Miriam N. Kotzin, author of *Debris Field* and *Country Music*, teaches literature and creative writing. Her novel, *Right This Way*, will be published by Spuyten Duyvil Press. Wiki *@miriam_n.kotzin*

November

My birthday falls in November, usually bleak and naked. But this November, many leaves, green, yellow, orange, and reddish-brown still cling to the branches. Tall asters flaunt their feathery purple petals along with the wild mums, pale pink, white and yellow. No leaves, no flowers, No-vember? Mother Nature prevails.

Kwan Kew Lai is an author, a Harvard medical faculty physician, an infectious disease specialist, a disaster response volunteer, an artist, and a runner. *kwankewlai.com*

It's Been a Hard Day's Recollection

The Fab Four, 1964, cavort across the silver screen. *They are so old!* sighs eleven-year-old me. Yesterday, Lovely Rita, Lady Madonna, Lucy in the Sky, and Eleanor Rigby, kept their faces in jars by the door. Still needed, still fed, my thoughts cavort at sixty-four, *They were so young!*

Linda M. Romanowski is a nonfiction writer and Italian hybrid memoir author with Sunbury Press. Twitter *@roman_leenda*

So Sorry!

A rush to exit the rapid ICE train, reaching for items, I hear "Sie haben meine Matel an." Screeching metal, shoving bodies, the same demand is voiced louder. A third time shouting! Turning sharply, I challenge … talking to me?

A meek response, "Yes, you have my coat on." Oops!

Deb Obermanns is an avid traveler, lover of storytelling, and international school teacher.

By the Canal

It's a glorious spring day after rain. Lucy takes the short cut along-side brightly painted barges, coots swimming with their chicks. The man grabs her from behind. She swivels, loose as a dancer, he slips in the fresh mud and tips over the edge. She stays to watch him drown.

Rosie Cullen lives in Manchester, UK, and likes writing all kinds of little stuff but still loves her big novel *The Lucky Country* best.

Fleeting

I know this time around, what I didn't truly know the first time—
it's fleeting.
The baby talk, the skinned knees.
Teenage eye rolls, mountains of laundry.
Closed doors, highs, and lows. Angst and triumphs.
  This time,
      I just pour
           out love like a fountain.
This time, I'm the Grandma.

Melissa Miles is a children's book author, certified educator, registered nurse, and
board chair of Superhero Success Foundation, Inc. Twitter *@melissajmiles*

The Dancer

Music and motion flow through stretched limbs. Tulle and tutus. Grace and beauty float —zephyr-like. Pointe shoes cover bloodied toes. Pain thrums every sinew. Hands poised, reaching. For what? Fame or fortune? No. Just the heartbeat of her life.

Apple Gidley, currently living in the Caribbean, is a global nomad who writes historical fiction, essays, and more. *applegidley.com*

Last Chapter of a Living Fairy Tale

When he sees his wife rousing from her nap, he flips the book open and recites the ending again. She blinks several times, slowly bringing his face and his voice into focus. Her apple-green eyes look no different now than the first time.

"I love that story," she says, smiling.

Bob Thurber is the author of six books. Over the years his work has received a long list of awards and been included in over sixty anthologies. *bobthurber.net*

The Baker

Her husband was a private investigator. She was a baker and made fresh donuts and cookies each morning for his clients. When he died, she took their daughter into her kitchen and taught her the recipes. "Cooking for someone," she said, "can be a way of giving comfort."

Morgan Want is a freelance writer, who has been writing since her teens, and is currently at work on her first novel. Instagram *@wantmorgan*

Middle Age

She wanted to throttle anyone who said, "Empty Nest Syndrome," as she grimaced a smile. Be less cliché, will you? Yes, the kids moved out, and she missed them. But just when she took a breath, her parents became old. How unfair was that?

A special education teacher by day, Theresa Milstein writes middle grade, YA, and dabbles in poetry. *theresamilstein.blogspot.com*

Carnival

When I turned up the carnival was over, and all the lights were out. I was hunting around to see if there was anything worth pocketing when someone, arms raised, came towards me from the sword-swallower's tent. A thud followed a woosh; my head ended up in this bucket.

Peter Snell was a bookseller, and he wears a lot of red in December. Facebook *@bartons.bookshop*

Love Bears It Away

My fingers trace the violence etched into your body. The pale incision that welcomed our first. This new scar, an exit wound made by the one we lost. And still you let me touch you, warm myself at your fierce fire? If that's not love, tell me what is.

Philip Feivel Wolff misspent his youth jamming in alternative rock bands and exploring the Smoky Mountains; these days he writes about horrors otherwise known as the real world. *fivewolff.weebly.com*

Dating

Finally, a date! A new dress: velour, hip-hugging, swale at the breast. Locket, he gave me on our anniversary. Hair frosted, his favorite style. He will watch me take my seat with newfound admiration, compelled to cry, "Don't leave! I love you!" Our first date all year—in court.

Shoshauna Shy lives in Madison, Wisconsin. *poetryumpsofftheshelf.com*

Blow the House Down

After her first husband nicknamed her "Porky," friends began giving pigs to Elizabeth on special and not-so-special occasions until they filled a kitchen shelf. "Porky loves those pigs," her husband would announce to visitors. Elizabeth dusted the pigs once more before locking the door behind her for the last time.

Now living in San Francisco, Laura Jacoby is an editor who writes for pleasure and pain. *jacobylm.net*

A Wild Drive

Wind, rain, and sleet battered Jessica's car as she navigated the deserted street, an obstacle course of fallen branches and rolling trash cans. A brilliant flash cut the inky sky. Body trembling, Jessica pulled into her unlit driveway. She sighed with relief when her therapist powered off the VR headset.

Rita Riebel Mitchell loves writing short fiction and the shorter the better. She is not a fan of thunderstorms. *ritariebelmitchell.com*

Sweetest Pain

He is cruel: rebuffing my affectionate touch. Unresponsive to the silent pleading in my loving eyes. His appetites all must be satisfied before he grudgingly allows—just briefly—the embrace of my hungry arms. Yet, I am beguiled more each day, tightly tethered to an inexplicably expanding love. Damnable puppy!

Jan Bartelli is a former journalist, a more-or-less retired attorney, and a less-is-more writer of creative nonfiction.

The Texas Beat: Part II

Her breath smelled like wet toast and gin. Upheaval makes for the best songs. It's not working out, getting your heart stomped on, the common theme. Theirs had become the archetypal musician crash and burn relationship. Hulks of twisted marital wreckage left to smolder on the west Texas horizon.

Living in Portugal agrees with Stuart Baker Hawk.

Mesmerizing

A respite. In search for a wider audience—my sisters, the sirens, have flown to Hollywood. They claim they're ready for *The Voice*. What for? They don't eat their prey anyway. Unless the audience is watching from their bathtubs there's little hope of the poor suckers drowning. —Medusa

Dale Champlin is a poet from Oregon who writes short stuff in long-hand. *champlindesign.com*

The Bear's Trip

A bear trips down Garrett Mountain, rolling haphazardly over golden grasses singed by the sun. The sun smiles in autumn form as days grow shorter and its fun sneaks vacantly away. The bear snorts, grimaces, pulls up on its torpid and aching haunches, and confronts its possibilities for the future.

R. Bremner writes of incense, peppermints, and the color of time.

Teapot

My twelve-year-old neighbor said, "I like the tiny pine tree you planted in that teapot." I took the opportunity to correct her.

"It is a pine tree, but it's in a teacup, not a teapot."

She smiled. "The minute you planted a tree in that cup, it became a pot."

Carol Keene is an artist and writer who romps gleefully in the right side of her brain. *carolkeene.com*

Birthday Party

Cake and sparklers adorn the festive table dressed for a celebration. Champagne glasses overflow with intoxicating refreshment. Voices harmonize the traditional song while gilded Florentine paper is torn revealing opulent offerings. Reality strikes: pandemic, war, famine, discrimination weigh heavily and the guilt of feeling happiness, steals another birthday.

Deb Obermanns is an avid traveler, lover of storytelling, and international school teacher.

The Sea Wall

I wondered if the sea wall on which the house was perched would give out on an ordinary day. It was a sunny Tuesday when all the talk was of Nor'easters and hurricanes, when the pounding of a million waves became too much. The concrete crumbled into the sea. Taking my daughter with it.

Sarah Canney has tried to make a career out of running and writing, even though she's an amateur.

The Comfort of a Constellation

I race into the darkness and flop on the damp grass; ignoring my foster mother's calls behind me. I need to find the Big Dipper, while there's a break in the clouds.

"There it is," I say, as it emerges from the mist. It's almost like Mama was still here.

Melissa Miles is a children's book author, certified educator, registered nurse, and board chair of Superhero Success Foundation, Inc. Twitter @*melissajmiles*

The Forgotten Years (Another Misadventure of the Broken Boys)

During the forgotten years the sun remained hidden for so long the boys took to measuring the passing of days by the depth of darkness. And even then, on nights when the moon shone bright, they trembled, fearful their own shadows knew disturbing secrets about the whereabouts of the sun.

Bob Thurber is the author of six books. Over the years his work has received a long list of awards and been included in over sixty anthologies. *bobthurber.net*

Unpacked

Was it just two years ago that the sisters had condensed the contents of a forty-year home into an assisted living apartment for their mother? This time, they packed to squeeze her life into a closet, dresser, and a nightstand. At age 82, Mom had her first roommate.

A special education teacher by day, Theresa Milstein writes middle grade, YA, and dabbles in poetry. *theresamilstein.blogspot.com*

Halftime

Time ticked on. He reached into his pocket, nothing. Sweat beaded. He checked again, nil. Frantically, he locked eyes with the nearest linesperson. They didn't speak the same language, but panic is universal. As he ran by, she reached out and discreetly pressed a whistle into his hand. Tweeeeeet!

Abiola writes poetry, fiction, and essays, and spends entirely way too much time going down '90s pop culture rabbit holes. Instagram *@arwriting*

How Time Flies

I stand beside a mountain pool, deep in reflective thought.

I notice a worn-out shirt sagging on a ragged stick.

"How did you find your way up this long meandering path?" I asked.

"You should know," he answered. "You are gazing at your own reflection."

Among other things, Paul Hertig has spent almost a lifetime playing with words. APU.edu @phertig

The Leftover's Contemplation

The one-third end of the tomato left over from lunch lies face-down on the saucer in the refrigerator, wondering if it will be cut up and tossed into a side salad for dinner, or diced into an omelet for breakfast. Three days later, it comes to grips with a third possibility.

Roy Dorman enjoys reading and writing speculative fiction and poetry.

A Night Out

My date for the night was slimmer than usual, which I put down to a sneaky corselet. Felicity's outfit was eye-popping: a frock covered in sequence with lateral coulisses, Doc Martens with six-inch heels and, to crown it all, a splendidly grotesque felt hat with purple violas and hanging participles.

JJ Toner was born under a gooseberry bush. He lives under a copper beech. *jjtoner.com*

The Dry Eye

The dry eye gets out of bed this morning, without the tears that usually drip from him. Today is finally not yesterday. It isn't yet tomorrow, but Time has learned again how to proceed. He thanks Time which relearned its duties, or, perhaps, decided to return early from its vacation.

R. Bremner's latest chapbook, *Erasing Influences*, is due in 2022 from Moonstone Arts Press.

Silver Alert

The notice appeared on the variable message board over the highway. Silver Alert. Be on the lookout for a Mercedes Benz C-43 AMG Turbo Convertible. Night Edition. Tag: Wildlife Federation WLDME. When I saw the alert, I laughed. They can find me, but they can't catch me.

Honey Rand has been writing since she could hold a pencil. Now she doesn't need to. *honeyrand.com*

The Inequities of Life

"She yanked her hair so hard her jaw wedged open. "This is my side," she hissed.

"Stop hurting me," she bellowed, in the hopes the authoritarians would hear and respond. "Your side is always bigger," she sobbed, her soul stinging from the inequities of life. Young sisters sharing a bed.

Shauna Lee Sanford McCarty enjoys writing and the daily belly laughter provided by her husband.

First Impression

"Meet your baby sister!" She holds the bundle out toward me.

Baby sister. These are new words. Curious but chary, I inch closer and catch a scent—new, yet somehow familiar. I soften. The bundle emits a shriek, blistering and monstrous. Ears back, I hiss and bolt from the couch.

Elizabeth Barton is a writer/editor living in Chicago with her husband, two cats, and more than a little self-doubt. *lizardesque.wordpress.com*

Kaibab Squirrel

The elusive Kaibab Squirrel scampers among the Ponderosa Pines isolated from other species. Adorable raven-black tummy, tufts of fur poke from its ears, a prize to photograph. Aperture professionally set to capture the sharpest image, burst mode engaged, successfully capturing ... one deadly bubonic carrying flea engorging on the host.

Deb Obermanns is an avid traveler, lover of storytelling, and international school teacher.

I Am

I have always been a late bloomer, buried under fuchsia petunias and cobalt lobelia, summer's instant celebrities. Exhausted, they wither in the cold dew, while I, the canary yellow dahlia, sway in the cracked clay pot and stretch my neck to kiss every ray of autumn sun.

Elizabeth Reed is writing a memoir about adventures like the leech attacks in Sumatra's jungles. *bettyreedwrites.com*

IGA

Her stepfather suggested the IGA parking lot. She scrolled her email as he hefted her mother's clothes into the trunk. "You can never have too many sweaters" read the Lee-Wrangler ad as he forced the lid closed. It seemed Mama had found a way to communicate from heaven after all.

Teri M. Brown works hard to connect readers to characters they'd love to invite to lunch. *terimbrown.com*

Language Lesson

My friend Pamela had no facility with foreign languages. But, as she was leaving to spend her two-week vacation in Athens, she cobbled together five Greek words and phrases she thought might come in handy: hello, please, thank you, you're very handsome, and kiss me. She had a wonderful time.

K. T. Maclay is an occasional writer living in the cultural center of Oaxaca de Juarez, Mexico.

Birthday Revenge

The earliest rays of sun dapple his stubbled jaw. It's been two hours since her text came. Rotten Cheat. I'd have left while he slept. Except it will be far more satisfying to let him see his birthday gift. Before I drive off in it. He'd always wanted a Tesla.

Melissa Miles is a children's book author, certified educator, registered nurse, and board chair of Superhero Success Foundation, Inc. Twitter *@melissajmiles*

Last Will and Testament

To my estranged daughter, who traveled across country for this reading, but couldn't attend my funeral, I bequeath one box of hugs. Though I hate to spoil a surprise or reveal a punchline I'll admit it's a crate filled with ravenous pythons waiting to squeeze the life out of you.

Bob Thurber is the author of six books. Over the years his work has received a long list of awards and been included in over sixty anthologies. *bobthurber.net*

Pickle

While raking up the leaves this autumn, I forgot a pile between the shed and fence. On Christmas Eve, I looked out the window and the leaves seemed different.

Pickle, one of our garden foxes, had patted the pile down. She was curled up, fast asleep, in her leaf nest.

Peter Snell was a bookseller, and he wears a lot of red in December. Facebook *@bartons.bookshop*

This Could've Been an Email

At the faculty meeting, she took notes about more unnecessary mandates from people in charge who probably had never taught in a classroom. She had to give them credit for rebranding of old ideas with new acronyms. Realization hit that education was an endless advertising campaign.

A special education teacher by day, Theresa Milstein writes middle grade, YA, and dabbles in poetry. *theresamilstein.blogspot.com*

Asphalt

Slick. Fast. Efficient. As Bertrand pulled off, a glance in the rearview mirror showed the body of the woman crumpled on the asphalt, her bag of groceries strewn around her. It'll look like a carjacking because it was a carjacking. And no more fucking alimony.

Joe Surkiewicz writes fiction in the Northeast Kingdom of Vermont.

Anonymity

Wet, white, and wild. The wind howls and whips snowflakes around. The snowflakes settle. As much as they look innocent, they'll be sure to leave the imprint of anyone who dares to cross them. Just wait. They'll be gone by morn and no one will suspect a thing.

LaKeshia is the author of *Wally's Dream* and loves to try her hand at all types of crafts.

Anesthesia

Trapped again by a rolling mass of glistening, odorous bodies, red finely stitching the white of my eyes, back muscles whimpering and guts quietly choking on ready-made trash, I squeeze my lids shut to summon your luminous, dawn-like face and feel no more discomfort, no anguish—nothing at all.

Tanya Petrova was born and raised in Ukraine but lives and works in Japan.

Ringing in the New Year

She chose one word per year to focus on. Something easily remembered and a good conversation starter. Mindfulness was a yawn, but promiscuity, especially if accompanied by eye candy on the arm, now that got a party started. As did levitation. Funny, how one word could raise a room's energy.

Joanne Nelson enjoys getting the party started. She is the author of *This Is How We Leave* and *My Neglected Gods. wakeupthewriterwithin.com*

Whatever He's Doing Down There

The magazines, piled thigh thick on the porch among spider webs 'til summer, include:

Popular Mechanics

Wild Game Kitchen

Do-It-Yourself Dungeons

Summoning for Beginners

Post-Apocalyptic Survival and You

Ritual Sacrifice Easy

Knives, Razors, Saws & More

Footsoldier of Discord

Pro Restraints

Come to think of it, I don't wanna know.

Genelle Chaconas is nonbinary, queer, is an abuse survivor, thrives with a mood disorder, is proud, enjoys cheap takeout, void screaming, drone/noise/industrial music, B-rated gangster and horror flicks, and long walks off short piers.

I'm Awake

It was dark but light. I turned onto my right side and touched her blonde hair. Outside, a car honked. A door slammed. Wheels wheeled away. The neighbor's dog barked. Red, orange, and yellow leaves stirred in the slight breeze. It was light but dark.

Tim Andersen is a Chicagoan. When he is not writing and reading, he travels, cooks, plays bridge, and bowls.

I Am Hope

Body bent and battered, limbs twisted under the weight of too many blows, the tree still stands. Still reaches its gnarled, gray bark upward toward the sun. Come springtime, newly sprouted twigs will stretch skyward, unfurling leaves in gilded light. "You thought your tempests could kill me. You were wrong."

Cordelia Frances Biddle's latest novel, *They Believed They Were Safe*, is available everywhere. *cordeliafrancesbiddle.net*

A Chance Meeting

They met unannounced on a jungle trail in '68, both instantly frozen in fear at the sight of the other. He fired fifteen rounds, and fifteen rounds were returned. Neither of them hit shit. They laughed as one at their foolishness and retreated into the bush. They would live to kill another day.

Steve Zettler is the author of *Careless Love. stevezettler.com*

The Yellow Blow-Up Duck Pool

I pace. The decking creaks. My dirty boots spill illusions. Renovation instructions muffle and reverberate the hot phone against my ear. I will not hear another word. Not about the yellow blow-up duck pool. They'll have to work around the last place his tiny soft feet splashed.

Jessica Bell's two-year-old son recently claimed that the banging of renovations was 'the heartbeat of building'. *iamjessicabell.com*

I Love You Daughter, and You are Mine

When Melinoe became of age, Hades disclosed truth: Zeus had raped Persephone; Melinoe's powers descended through Zeus's bloodline, not his own. She commanded ghosts that could drive anyone insane, through daydreams or nightmares. So Melinoe plagued Zeus with demented hauntings. His madness descended until Hera hid him away: sweetest vengeance.

By day, Kathryn teaches; by night, she resurrects gods, goddesses, folk, and fairy tales. Twitter *@katecanwrite*

Rwandan Remembrance

How to explain how my hometown fell apart and my family fled? I had loved my home, where I played in the fields with my sisters and brothers. Everybody was friendly. A mirage. One assassination, one plane shot from the sky, and the streets were filled with neighbors killing neighbors.

Gretchen Cowell is the author of the parents' guide *Help for the Child with Asperger's Syndrome*, and enjoys writing historical fiction.

I Want to Break Free

I'm stuck, hung up on this stupid sticky vessel wall in the left leg. Boring! I'll probably dissolve before I get to have any fun. In daydreams, I break loose and ride the current toward thrilling, exotic locations: heart, lung, brain—places where I can really fuck some shit up.

Elizabeth Barton is a writer/editor living in Chicago with her husband, two cats, and more than a little self-doubt. *lizardesque.wordpress.com*

Lonely Town

In a desert town with no buildings, and no bearings on a map, the only structure was a sign: the town's population. A line of blood crossed out the '1' in the middle of the sign, and a track of bloody footsteps reached as far as the eye could see.

Kaiya Sothern comes from New Zealand and runs her own candy store. Instagram *@human.no.13*

The Cloud

"You realize that 'the cloud' is just a server farm, right?" The teenager stopped typing on her mobile phone and looked over at the old man as though he'd just told her that the earth was flat. Then she pensively glanced skyward.

Phillip Temples, of Watertown, Massachusetts, has published five mystery-thriller novels, a novella, and two short story anthologies in addition to over 160 short stories online. *temples.com*

The Fairground

An opaque fog engulfs the field. Muffled notes from a military band faintly permeate the damp air. Shadowy soldiers, rifles, and horses blur the foreground, yet a foreboding energy refracts outward. My companion barks frantically into the void, retreating. A spine-chilling glance backward and the silhouette brown shirts vanish.

Deb Obermanns is an avid traveler, lover of storytelling, and international school teacher.

Whiskers on Kittens

In my living room sits a large, round, willow bowl full of kittens. No, not real kittens; fluffy, cuddly, toy ones. My younger grandchildren enjoy playing with them. I wore them to a singalong showing of *The Sound of Music*. They were joined together as a scarf beneath my beard.

Peter Snell was a bookseller, and he wears a lot of red in December. Facebook *@bartons.bookshop*

Horror

In the cemetery, the night was cold and tree leaves shuffled in the breeze. I saw a lady with electric hair across the Fewa Lake. She held a hammer and chisel and pounded on a gravestone. I asked what she was doing. She said, "they spelt my name wrong!"

Santosh Kalwar works as a poet, writer, and researcher. His stories, poems have appeared in various places. *kalwar.com.np*

Someone Get the Real Sheriff

Sheriff continued to drink as the fight around him escalated. Chairs crashed through glass. Men bounced across the bar. The working girls upstairs hollered for folks to keep it down. Nobody minded the mangy dog in the corner slurping from his bowl of water, just as round two began.

Raymond Sloan lives in Ireland with wife, Jolene, and daughter, Lottie.

Did You See That Times Piece?

"Did you see that Times piece about ..."

"You know I only watch comedies and only read books about summer," she interrupted, intent on the paint-by-number before her.

"Yes," he restarted, "but ..."

"And why," she continued, "does everything you want to say to me require that I have read the Times?"

Emmy-award-winner Amy Bass is a writer, professor, and sport thinker. *amybass.net*

Ukraine

I studied the night sky seeking solace ... Sagittarius, Orion, Aries, and the Pleiades were brilliantly shining down at the chaos unraveling beneath them. Constellations withstanding time, dependable, constant guards; the still of the moment shattered by explosions! A meteorite streaked across the horizon: like a lone falling tear pledging solidarity.

Deb Obermanns is an avid traveler, lover of storytelling, and international school teacher.

Lost on Sicilian Roads

Lost, we stop in a village. Ask smoker outside a Bar for directions. Can't understand him. Many others come out, no luck. Finally, old man hobbles out. "Was WW-II American prisoner, taken to Texas". I think *Oh darn, here anger comes!*

He says, "Was the best time of my life!"

Pete Obermanns is a retired Navy helicopter pilot, who joined to see the world and has been to forty-four countries so far. He hopes to complete his memoir before he's completed.

Fractured Heart

Lump in throat: heart finding a new home. Sweaty palms: could mean anything. Ache in belly: could be gas. Brain sore: a bruise that I can't stop fiddling with. My heart hangs on a branch—a ripe plum. Squeezed, sniffed, prodded. There to be loved; there to be broken.

Amie McCracken edits and typesets novels for self-published authors and helps writers polish their work. *amiemccracken.com*

July Baby

Every year it rained on her birthday. Twenty-seven years of planning indoor celebrations became the norm. This year rebelling against the expected, hopeful for cloudless blue skies, optimistic for dry leafy terrains, she arranges a horseback riding trip for us.

This year the Universe gifts her with a tornado.

Jass Aujla plans perfect (fictional) murders in-between her day-job meetings. *jassaujla.com*

Light Bulb Moment

They're having a hot steamy love-making session on a sweltering afternoon in Florence. Smiling, he's looking down at her, thinking *live together, then a short engagement (maybe a year or two), then marriage, children.* Smiling, she's looking up right past him, thinking *my aunt has that light shade.*

Ellen Fox is an award-winning playwright, who has also written for radio, film, and television.

Excuse Me

As she pushed her way through the swell of Axe-Body-sprayed students pouring from classrooms and clustering at lockers, she wished to be taller. Remembering that long-ago promise to herself that she'd never set foot in a middle school again left a bitter after-taste. That was before she became a teacher.

A special education teacher by day, Theresa Milstein writes middle grade, YA, and dabbles in poetry. *theresamilstein.blogspot.com*

Dreams Unfulfilled

"This isn't what I had hoped would happen," she whispered—
although it was what she'd feared the most all along. At least since
the diagnosis. She folded his hands lovingly onto his chest and
kissed his forehead. Knowing life would never be as rich again.

Melissa Miles is a children's book author, certified educator, registered nurse, and
board chair of Superhero Success Foundation, Inc. Twitter *@melissammiles*

She is Nice

Passengers crowd the gate, unexplained delay. Boarding
commences; customers shove to claim limited space. The seats
stuffed with bodies resembling exhausted stevedores. Cabin secure
and two out of three vacant seats remain! Turning aft, "Are you a
nice person?"

A perky response, "Yes, I believe so!" Serendipity made them
friends.

Deb Obermanns is an avid traveler, lover of storytelling, and international
school teacher.

Squash

That Sunday morning was the first time that I had beaten my father at squash.

I went off with my other half to celebrate at the Pub. When we got back the undertaker had already driven off with his body in a temporary fiberglass coffin. Talk about a hollow victory.

Peter Snell was a bookseller, and he wears a lot of red in December. Facebook *@bartons.bookshop*

The Photograph

I stroke the scalloped edges of the black and white photo from a Brownie flash camera. A glue-backed piece of paper is stuck across her face. But I know she is wearing rhinestone cat's eyeglasses and a white, sleeveless dress. Because I still remember our first kiss.

Zvi A. Sesling, Brookline, MA Poet Laureate (2017-2020), has published numerous poems and flash fiction.

A Sailor's Resolve

Moonlight sparkled the bay.

Hoyt announced, "I can't race tomorrow. Gotta cracked hull."

Skipper cracked a beer. "Tank's crew is strong."

Hoyt froze. He swigged as a video game chirped. Tank had just married his ex. Diamond big as a beer nut. Hoyt began to brainstorm.

"I got an idea."

Cesca Janece Waterfield is the author of three poetry collections and a forthcoming memoir. *cescawaterfield.wordpress.com*

Gum be Gone

After chewing gum, pre-teen Jimmy stuck it behind his ears. His dark, thick hair hid all signs of it neatly. Only once the gum dried and fell onto his shoulder and then the floor. His friends saw and laughed, so now Jimmy swallows his gum to be safe.

Norbert Kovacs lives and writes in Hartford, Connecticut. *norbertkovacs.net*

The Rocks She Carried

Geraldine glared at the Mississippi, the Arch towering beside her. Voices judged: classmates calling her stupid, her brother calling her ugly. She once ignored them, but today Mike's "let's be friends" scattered resilience to the wind. Hoping the rocks in her pockets would be enough, she stepped from the bridge.

Sally Simon has visited St. Louis and has even gone up the Arch, but ze hails from the Catskills in NY State. *sallysimonwriter.com*

Blue on White

Stay back! My cap point menaced, as I screeched at the trespassers. Mine! Wings spread and thrumming with purpose, I swooped in arcs, ever closer, from branch to icy branch. Then, in a dizzy drop with an indigo flash, I pounced on the snow and claimed my blueberry prize. Joy.

J.H. Jones, new to writing about what takes her fancy, likes to watch the backyard birds.

Searching

The English waitress was wearing a scarf today.

"You look different. Is it significant?"

"Yes." Then, defensively, "I'm happy with my decision."

So much I could say, so little I should. Instead, the usual Arabic greeting escapes my lips.

"You took this journey?" she asks, shocked.

"Yes, there and back."

Karen Al-Ghabban is a lover of words and languages, and she is married with two children and two dogs.

Good Ol' USA

No more begging on the median breathing car exhaust, sleeping under the Ellston Street bridge. Even though COVID took my job, I scored free medical care, three meals a day, bed, and a roof over my head. All it took was killing a man on duty for the postal service.

Shoshauna Shy is a poet, flash fiction editor, and cat care provider. *poetryjumpsofftheshelf.com*

Dite

Dite. Like Aphrodite. Meant to be mispronounced unless you're in on it. I was never invited to meet her but knew enough for her biography.

"Her parents are doctors," my husband said casually, leaving. "Educated family."

Should've thrown my pasta at him. Instead, I groaned "How erudite" and got blitzed.

Jenna Brown is a writer and designer based in Portland, Oregon. *qbcreative.com*

Giant

The Superintendent gave the order: "Secure the scene, lads."

"Move along, folks," the Inspector shouted. "Nothing to see here."

"Do we have a name?" said the sergeant, climbing a ladder.

"Lemuel Gulliver," replied someone in the crowd.

"We're gonna need a lot more chalk," said the patrolman.

JJ Toner was born under a gooseberry bush and lives under a copper beech. *jjtoner.com*

Per Chance

The croupier nods hello. "How's it going tonight?"

"Not so good," she says. A small grimace, followed by an abashed, yet hopeful, smile. "But you know what they say–'past performance is no indicator of future results.'"

He smiles and rakes his stick across the craps table.

"Wanna bet?"

Jan Bartelli is a former journalist, a more-or-less retired attorney, and a less-is-more writer of creative nonfiction.

Middle School

The stupid boys, drenched in Axe Body Spray, tossed her hat over her head. An unjust punishment for trying to infuse a little fashion into their blending-in uniform. Now, along with acne and braces, she'd have to endure the day with hat hair.

A special education teacher by day, Theresa Milstein writes middle grade, YA, and abbles in poetry. *theresamilstein.blogspot.com.*

The House Was Mine

The man who ran the estate sale left the house broom clean as promised. But he couldn't sweep away the ghosts: unfaded rectangles on the walls; a wine stain like old blood; a dent where someone broke a knuckle. My thoughtful daughter dropped me off. I could sob in peace.

Chet Ensign writes from northern New Jersey where he just painted the house.

Sunlight

In June I hooked up with the King of Promises. In July I was still the kind of girl who could say "fortuitously" without irony. In August I learned how to count myself lucky. Loving him I found the key to unlock the secret of happiness. Expect little, want less.

Miriam N. Kotzin, author of *Debris Field* and *Country Music*, teaches literature and creative writing. Her novel, *Right This Way*, will be published by Spuyten Duyvil Press.

Embers

The old man believed calamity lurked, waiting to catch one unaware. He lived on high alert for the sound of laughter or song, critical of luminosity in a dark world. His wife struggled to repress a soul that found brilliance in the darkness, lest her husband find fault in an ember of hope.

Barbara Elliott is a Philadelphia-based artist, writer, and lover of baseball.

Wild West Romance

As Jake rode, he wondered how to ask her. No great shakes with words, so he just out with it. She didn't say no. Suddenly, lightning cracked, and the herd spooked. He galloped to head them off, his black hat sailing away on the wind.

Doug Jacquier is an Australian legend in his own lunchtime and a former rock band roadie (which explains a lot).

Metafiction

"How about a 50 Give or Take about a writer who can't think of an idea for a flash piece?" Ian typed.

"Eh," Jessica responded without enthusiasm.

"You already did that in your novel."

Ian opened the email, blinked twice, then stared at his laptop in defeat.

Ian M. Rogers has a really funny novel about writing called *MFA Thesis Novel* published by Vine Leaves Press. *ianmrogersauthor.com*

Missing Justice

What Caleb needed was a miracle. But, ever since Justice moved out, miracles had been in short supply. He pounded his fist on the table. "Why do I mess everything up?" he shouted. Taking a deep breath, he punched his boss's number into his phone. "Let me explain," he began.

Melissa Miles is a children's book author, certified educator, registered nurse, and board chair of Superhero Success Foundation, Inc. *Twitter @MelissaJMiles*

Shootout in the Old West

"This town ain't big enough for the both of us."

"You ornery sidewinder! 'Ol' Benny will count to three and we'll draw."

"One ... Two ... Three!!!"

Two men lay in the dirt, looking up at the sky with unseeing eyes.

"I'll be danged if the town don't seem a bit bigger," said Benny.

Roy Dorman enjoys reading and writing speculative fiction and poetry.

Neighborly Love

She pushed and pulled the sofa, turning it around to face the window before opening her curtains. What a view, she thought. That night, she sipped wine and munched popcorn in the dark, watching the neighbors across the alley as they undressed each other, swaying to music she couldn't hear.

Rita Riebel Mitchell writes at home and on road trips with her husband. She enjoys reading and writing short and very short fiction. *ritariebelmitchell.com*

The Perils of Forgetfulness

Derek was known for being forgetful. He always used to keep dupli-
cate house and car keys at his friends' pads. He really seemed to
have his life—and his little problem—under control. How he forgot
to strap on his parafoil before stepping off the cliff we will never
know.

Peter Snell was a bookseller, and he wears a lot of red in December. Facebook
@bartons.bookshop

Assisted Suicide

My good-byes are said. The order is signed, the IV hooked up. The
doctor comes in, the vial in his hand. Last chance to say *No*. To spend
last painful months with my distraught daughter, my hand pressed
by my overwhelmed lover, or, in just seconds, let it all go.

Gretchen Cowell lives in Philadelphia and loves reading and writing.

Nor'easter

At midnight, it arrived silently and softly, drifting, dreamy, white fluff from heaven. A lone crepuscular bunny scampered along, barely leaving any footprints. Overnight, it came down fast and furious, gusting wind transformed the gentle snowfall into a blizzard, embracing our world with its swirling, blinding whiteness of purity.

Kwan Kew Lai is an author, a Harvard medical faculty physician, an infectious disease specialist, a disaster response volunteer, an artist, and a runner. *kwankewlai.com*

Jumping with Scissors

The foul tempered younger sister refuses to heed sibling guidance. Vigorously engaged in nonsense she jumps on the bed, imitating a pirate slicing the airy enemy with a pair of scissors. The resulting scar left by the embedded shears, provides the first indication of a lifetime of preventable errors.

Deb Obermanns is an avid traveler, lover of storytelling, and international school teacher.

Errands

"Sorry I'm late hun. I had some errands to run after work."

"You must be beat. Let me get you a drink."

"I'm also a little spooked. I had the feeling I was being followed."

"That was me following you on your way to your errands' apartment. Like your drink?"

The author, Doug Hawley, is short. Google *@aberrantword*

Counting The Beans

She watches the fugue erupt. Her sister's blue eyes at sea with the world. That moment green turned to amber, then to red, when the counting and waiting began. The sobbing child feels safe beside her sister, hears her heartbeat. The man lights a cigarette, tight lipped.

Jenny writes each day and makes abstract ceramics.

Scrambled Eggs

He is no longer robust. We laugh at the squeaky walker. The sound is funny, his need for it is not. He wants to be helpful, so he washes the dishes. I thank him and, when he can't see, flick missed detritus off the plates. Thumbnail clean is good enough.

Deborah Jones is a dyed-in-the-wool New Englander learning to bloom where she's planted in the Midwest. It's been fifty years.

Panic Attack

Adrenaline pumps through my veins. My heart rate skyrockets. I seek escape, protection, a safe haven. But with each signal, each terrified reaction, my rational brain asks, "Can I trust it?" Is this sunny day, waiting in line for an ice cream, really a threat to my existence?

Amie McCracken edits and typesets novels for self-published authors and helps writers polish their work. *amiemccracken.com*

A is for Attitude

She attempted Ben Franklin's thirteen virtues ("Temperance, Silence, Order, Resolution ..."), but she had insufficient Resolution. Then she tried an abecedarian, adjusting her Attitude and upgrading her "B" and "C," to Busy and Cheerful; however, she overplayed Determined and backslid to Difficult. Her friends liked her better Drunk and Easy.

Miriam N. Kotzin, author of *Debris Field* and *Country Music*, teaches literature and creative writing. Her novel, *Right This Way*, will be published by Spuyten Duyvil Press.

What a Great Space!

"Wow, what a great space!" Suzy enthused.

"You want to take a look in the next room!" grinned the realtor.

Suzy opened the door full of excited anticipation. It was pitch black. She stepped through and fell, hurtling past a luminous moon, spinning planets and floating stars.

"Heavens!" she exclaimed.

Rosie Cullen lives in Manchester, UK, and likes writing all kinds of little stuff but still loves her big novel *The Lucky Country* best.

Maximalist & Hostages

Hate to call it a day so early and go back to the empty apartment with the broken heater, so I keep the conversation rolling beyond its natural lifespan, filling pauses, posing questions no one cares much about, chasing fellow merry-makers to their vehicles when they try to retreat politely.

Todd Mercer writes fiction and poetry in Grand Rapids, Michigan, and he loves this life.

Marriage

The ramen was delicious going down— not so much coming up. I vomited it into the toilet, and it vomited it back out at me. Both of us overflowing, I heaved into a spare Walmart bag, laughing at the absurdity. My husband, naked and plunging, looked at me with love in his eyes: "Can you please shut the fuck up?"

Sara Watkins is a full-time developmental editor, part-time author, and freelance collector of tiny, fat dragons—no one pays her to collect them, she just enjoys it. *sarawatkins.net*

Flowers of Precipitation

Thursday came his dream: she was on the floor, covered in blood, and he was bending over her. Friday brought flowers. He was still trying to decide. Saturday, lightheaded, she got up in the night to pee. Get down! She thought.

But she didn't get down fast enough.

Lorri McDole's writing has appeared in Flash Nonfiction Funny, The Writer, Prime Number Magazine, Cleaver, Sweet, The Offing, Talking Writing, and many other places. *@lorrimcdole*

Night Owl

An owl's hunting cry awakens Rufus who barks until I take him outside. Rufus shrinks back until he sees owl fly off. Then, he pulls me through the grass where frogs and crickets are still in chorus. Their melodies sing us back to sleep when we return inside.

Joan Leotta tells tales on page and stage. Facebook *@joanleotta*

Goodbye, Girls

They'd been with her through thick and thin, albeit less prominent during the thin. They were part of her—figuratively and literally. A cheek swab had revealed the lurking threat: BRCA1-positive. At the mirror, she gazed at her unclad torso, bid them a silent goodbye, then donned the hospital gown.

Elizabeth Barton moves words around for fun and profit while living in Chicago with her husband, two cats, and more than a little self-doubt. *lizardesque.wordpress.com*

OCD

One by one, she stretches each vertebra before her feet hit the cold morning floor. Two, four, six, eight steps to the bathroom. Ten, twelve, fourteen, steps to the stairs, plus thirteen steps total twenty-seven. "Stop counting," she soothes, "It's exhausting,". Deep breath.

Then mismatched light switches demand her attention.

Shauna Lee McCarty enjoys writing and the daily laughter provided by her husband.

To the Sea

It was her friend, her priestess, her everything. And she had to be with it; inside of it. At night it was too dangerous. But, when morning cracked across the wide sky, she could go. Barefoot, she ran over the sand, reached its edge, and dropped to her knees.

Benjamin Jelkmann lives with his wife and writes from somewhere or other, and always temporarily. Facebook *@benjamin.jelkmann*

Brutal Honesty, or, Ways to Say "I Love You"

"Make me Cottage Pie, and Lasagna, Mum," pleads teenage daughter.

"Did you miss me, darling?"

"Oh, yes. A week without your food is too much ... Actually, can you write them down please, with pictures?"

"Are you preparing for your children?"

"No, I'm preparing for when you're dead!"

Karen Al-Ghabban is a lover of words and languages, and she is married with two children and two dogs.

Ringing in the New Year

Every affair has moments of extreme bliss in an infinity of dread.

Getting dressed, Jack was in panic mode. "Where's my ring? I can't go home without my wedding band."

Suddenly realizing all that was at stake, Jack was stricken. Rachel wore a smile of hope during her half-hearted search.

Bill Diamond lives in the Rocky Mountains of Colorado where he writes to try and figure it all out.

Mrs. Edwards

My memory of the pharmacist's wife is one of gaiety, her chic black coat and great hat, a nest of swirly voile. That tremulous soprano voice, blue eyes, sapphires piercing to the epicenter. I wonder what made her fall? Her own daydream perhaps, a moment's distraction? Eau de toilette?

Jenny writes each day and makes abstract ceramics.

A Restless Night

After many restless hours I woke and checked my watch: 2:56. I went back to sleep; waking up, unrested, at 5:12. Later, making a hot drink in the kitchen, I saw a fox trotting across the lawn. I checked my watch, which showed 10:24. This is how memories are saved.

Peter Snell was a bookseller, and he wears a lot of red in December. Facebook *@bartons.bookshop*

When Time Stood Still

Before the crash, a gray sedan traveling in the westbound lane, hit the median curb, launching itself off the shady pavement, into the late afternoon sunshine. The vehicle's bumper glistened about ten feet from my windshield, with its hood ornament aiming at my once-perfect life.

Carol Keene is a fine art painter who, when she cannot paint, resorts to words to create images.

In the Nick

There is progress in the process. The crews toiled with blizzard speed, monkeying between branches. They risked life to cut limbs. They stumped the trees, lumbering them. "Why the rush?" I asked. What if the ominous omnibus missed?

Allison Whittenberg is a poet and novelist. Her latest work is *Carnival of Reality* from Loyola University Press.

Pilot's Message

"May I have your attention!" The passengers, white-knuckled, jaws clenched, listened intently to the crackling message, as stomachs roared into their throats.

"A show of hands. How many wish they'd listened to the safety lecture? April Fool's."

Chuckling uproariously, he righted the plane, putting it on auto-pilot again.

Teri M. Brown, debut author of *Sunflowers Beneath the Snow*, connects readers to characters they'd love to invite to lunch. *terimbrown.com*

Rumor Has It

The shopkeeper notes the new guy in town simply pays, nods, and leaves. Clearly, he's had throat cancer and he's come here to recover. He never visits the bar. The owner concludes he is an alcoholic drying out. Rumor has it that silent invisibility is a hit man's best weapon.

Doug Jacquier is an Australian who writes stories and poems. *sixcrookedhighwaysblog.wordpress.com*

Good Tomato

Climbing the dusty cobblestones reciting the Italian greeting in her head,
Buon Pomeriggio; Good Afternoon. Rereading the well-scripted grocery list she
enters the village store prepared, getting the order requested perfectly! Proudly
departing she proclaims, "Buon Pomodoro Tutti!"
The clerks smile, proclaiming
"Good Tomato to You Signora Deborah!"

Deb Obermanns is an avid traveler, lover of storytelling, and international school teacher.

The Bus Stop

3:05, Arriving at the bus stop, I lean provocatively against the tiny shelter until the man gives me his seat.

3:25, Rain starts, soaking the man.

3:30, I let him sit, squeezed up against me.

3:40, Hail starts. "Give us a kiss," the man asks. The stakes keep getting higher.

Gretchen Cowell lives in Philadelphia and loves historical fiction.

Dinner-Date Disaster

His sweaty palms and pits almost gave him away. Apprehension overtook his body causing an uncharacteristic stutter. He reached for her hand, toppling his wine glass. Burgundy liquid flowed across the table onto her lap. Horrified, he quickly pulled the small box from his pocket and dropped to one knee.

Rita Riebel Mitchell writes tiny bits of fiction every day—some of it is published, some of it floats in the cloud.

Perks of Adulthood

Lifting a bowl to lick out that last morsel of food would have occasioned a sharp tsk-tsk from my mother. Now, here I sit contemplating a small mound of pasta that won't get on the fork. I chase it around the rim. Heck, she's gone, and I'm in my seventies. You know what happens next. Delicious!

Deborah Jones likes red wine, wombats, and Oxford commas. Not necessarily in that order.

Dichotomies

Men in suits look and turn away. She sees her aging reflection in the venue's bar mirror. Again, instantly invisible due to facial lines and thinning lips. The crowd is seated, two minutes her assistant cues. She adjusts her Spanx and scans her presentation notes: *Sexuality, Self-Worth, & the Aging Feminist.*

Shauna Lee McCarty enjoys writing and the daily laughter provided by her husband.

Eyeshadow

Her teen boy was proud, gay. Naive of hatred, judgement: he painted his handsome face. Together, navigating and aching over his first hateful attack. His defeated spirit wept strength, kindness, pure love. Protection from discrimination, tucking him away.

"Don't wear your rainbow too vividly, son."

Bravely, he re-applied eyeshadow.

Jade Visone writes with soul-filled honesty about the struggles and magic of mothering, love, life, dandelions, and stars.

Little Peeper

The girl fidgeted on the stool, leaning toward the keyhole. She could see their TV screen, smell cigarettes, hear music. A man, woman, kisses. Drama! She felt clever, watching grown-up movies like this after bedtime, not knowing her mom could always hear her. Until she decided it was enough.

Nina Lichtenstein, a writer, teacher, and storyteller, was born and raised in Oslo, Norway, but divides her time between Maine, USA, and Tel Aviv, Israel. *ninalichtenstein.com*

Granny's Last Day

On Monday evening, Granny ironed Pawpaw's striped pajamas.

"What are you doing, dear? You don't feel well; go upstairs."

"I'm not letting my husband go to bed with wrinkled clothes. I'll iron, if it's the last thing I do!" Tuesday night, Papaw's pajamas matched his skin.

Bethany Jarmul is a writer, essayist, and mom from Pittsburgh. Twitter: *@bethanyjarmul*

Door Number One

The door opens, and the monster sucks David's memories like a hose vacuuming dust. Abandoned plans, broken loves, even the trivial: the face of the assistant librarian, a shattered glass in Reykjavik, that jigsaw puzzle with the missing piece. Perhaps the monster can build a better life from the clutter.

Chuck Augello is the author of *The Revolving Heart*, a Best Books of 2020 selection by Kirkus Reviews. *cda.thedailyvonnegut.com*

Blossoming Romance

Shruthi planted her seed of love for him in a small pot. Passion took root. Watered by desire, he sprouted. A green tendril poked through fertile soil, reaching toward her. To nurture him, captivating, though he held the potential to be a clinging vine as much as a vibrant bloom.

Nina Miller is happily married to a mighty oak tree for nearly twenty-five years. *ninamillerwrites.com*

Date with a Pretty Thing

Thick eyelashes rise and fall like sparrow wings-- darting and yet graceful. Brown eyes stare out at nothing while long, elegant fore and middle fingers fiddle with the salt shaker. Full lips are slightly parted. You haven't said anything. Not yet. You're waiting. You just want to look for now.

Azizat Danmole is an Illinois-hearted Missourian who writes, instructs writing, and counsels young people. Facebook *@adanmole*

Feline Believer

I slump in the chair after another sleepless night, smoothing the wrinkled funeral brochure in my knotted hands. My faith shaken, I ask, "Why?" Whiskers, hopeful, sits in the bay window. His eyes following a bird's wings as it rises toward a lemonade sunrise. Does my cat believe in God?

Ann S. Epstein, whose height in inches is roughly commensurate with this story's length in words, writes fiction and memoir. *asewovenwords.com*

She Didn't Take the Bait

The sinuous serpent hissed temptations to Eve when a worm writhed out of the forbidden fruit. She grimaced, then gagged. Thanks to her aversion to creepy-crawly things, Adam, Eve, and all mankind were saved. On the other hand, the slimy worm, with belly full, was forever banned from Paradise.

Ruth Mannino likes to imagine different endings to common myths.

The Last Tinsmith in Kagoshima

The old man rises from lunch to greet a cramped storefront for a tall tourist. Crafting so many vessels until there is no shelf left—a lineage realized but usually unsold. The hammered precision of two tin cups stored in a condominium cupboard an ocean away, a passing immortality.

Kevin presumes to write in Vancouver, Canada.

It's The Sudden Stop

The cable snaps at the fifty-third floor. The car's descent is slow—initially. At forty-two, the life flash starts—Sunday breakfast, summer camp, Uncle Frank's psoriasis, first kiss, last kiss. Floor fifteen: you smell bacon and skin cream. You realize it's not the fall that kills you.

E. O'Neill is a New Jersey native that watches the world but rarely participates.

A Close Bathe

In my tin bath, in my tent, in the jungle, in Burma I was unprepared for the Japanese attack on our camp. Hunkered down, I heard and felt bullets hitting the metal. Afterwards, I found my clothes, left on the back of a chair, were full of new moth holes.

Peter Snell was a bookseller, and he wears a lot of red in December. Facebook *@bartons.bookshop*

A Hate-Filled Void

I was twelve when Jill's body became broken beyond repair. I knew she wasn't getting back up. I also knew it was my fault—my idea to bike that hill. I didn't know the extent one person could hate another. Yet I still see her mother's face, contorted with rage.

Melissa Miles is a children's book author, certified educator, registered nurse, and board chair of Superhero Success Foundation, Inc.

Midnight Dance

A deserted graveyard. Hours before somber people had gathered. I was not one of them. Reading his name, scribbled on a simple cross filled me with joy. The soil shifted under my feet, as if I was in danger of joining him, but it held, and I danced until dawn.

Lee Montgomery-Hughes is a full time logophile (lover-of-words) and totally addicted to the art of stringing them together. *leemontgomery.weebly.com*

Poet Marries Engineer

She wanted houses for their witch caps, wainscotted pantries, or pink clawfoot tubs. He disqualified any from consideration due to water-stained cellars or jerry-rigged wiring. By house fifteen, she let him go in first. A subsequent nod at the screen door signaled Yup—get your hopes up!

Shoshauna enjoys being with trees, books, cats, chocolate, and her husband, preferably all at the same time. *catsittersecrets.com*

Shakespeare Would Laugh

They practiced their Shakespearean lines adding classical Baroque music to enrich the scene. "Oh here, oh here" was all he was assigned to deliver to the audience. Deeply exhaling he bellows, "Oh cow, Oh cow!" Stunned, the young actor, questions what just happened? The lunch bell rings, Burgers!

Deb Obermanns is an avid traveler, lover of storytelling, and international school teacher.

A Now

I count the moments, shoals of them as they brush base, beginning to make acceptance a possibility, a reminder there is elegance in an empty room, clear light on wooden floors, pianos.

Jenny writes each day and makes abstract ceramics.

Love Letter

Thank you for understanding the dark depths of it; for inviting me to your home full of laughter and never-ending food; for a study space fashioned from two file cabinets and a slab of marble; for offering the normal that forever seemed mythological; for love without rope burns.

A special education teacher by day, Theresa Milstein writes middle grade, YA, and dabbles in poetry. *theresamilstein.blogspot.com*

The Prima Ballerina

Turning in perfect circles, her eyes focus on the Garden Fairy's green dress to stay balanced. She wears the audience's applause like a shield against her. When the circle breaks, the Garden Fairy stands. A chorus of running feet vibrates against in her body like a metronome.

Morgan Want is a former journalist, who has been writing since her teens. She is currently at work on her first novel. Instagram *@wantmorgan*

All Change

Our rainbow baby was five months old when Daddy married on a moonlit African shore. Guests cheered as he plunged the knife into the sponge castle, unaware he'd crossed the Meridian Line with a suitcase of second-hand silk and deceit. I do, I say, as the locksmith changes the lock.

Nicky loves short fiction and lives in a lively English seaside town with her son. *diamond-minds.co.uk*

Sunday Dinner

Should she bring something?

Yes, bring something, Nan's stern voice in her head.

What do they even like?

Make something you like.

She's got desiccated blueberries, two organic eggs.

Limes in a teak bowl that match the table-runner's green.

Pie?

Maybe.

The recipe says *Key* Lime. What's the key part?"

Melanie Faith is a night-owl writer and editor who often moves through the daytime world with her camera and heart-shaped, leopard-print sunglasses. *melaniedfaith.com*

Gum Love

It wasn't meant to happen. I asked for his help with a phantom leak around my air conditioner. He fiddled around, scratched his head, took a stick of gum from his shirt pocket, chewed, used it to plug the hole. I suppose I've fallen in love for worse reasons.

Judith Shapiro secretly writes flash fiction, when the novel she's writing looks the other way.

Unseen Messages

She said she received messages from above. They are unseen messages clear to her mind about war, drugs, killing, NBA playoffs. She made her predictions: a war, synthetic drugs, serial killers, Lakers winning the championship. That was last year. This year her mind received no messages.

Zvi A. Sesling, Brookline, MA Poet Laureate (2017-2020), has published numerous poems, flash fiction and short stories.

The Order of the Factors Does Alter the Product

Norman was always a bit disorganized. He had set three purposes in life: plant a tree, have a child, and write a book. Finally, after much trying, he succeeded, in his own way: he wrote a tree, planted a son, and had a book. Now Norman is disorganizedly satisfied.

Marcelo Medone is a writer from Buenos Aires, Argentina whose flash fiction story "Last Train to Nowhere Town" has been nominated for the 2021 Pushcart Prize. @marcelomedone

Back Home

I walked off the wooden dock and into the pine grove up ahead. I saw the ruby-red rays piercing through the trees, and I inhaled the sweet scent of pine roasting in the twilight that pulsates through the heavy air. That's when I knew I was home.

Benjamin Jelkmann lives with his wife and writes from somewhere or other, and always temporarily. Facebook @benjamin.jelkmann

Habituated Suffocation

"I'm leaving." Her words rang down the hall. Memories consumed him. First kiss. Leisurely morning coffees. That spiraling glint of hair at the nape of her neck. His mind raged, "I won't let it end!"

"Need anything at the store?" she called, stepped outside, checked her list, and left.

Shauna Lee Sanford McCarty enjoys writing and finding reasons to laugh.

Fall From Grace

She appeared, a "suggested friend." Still beautiful, and very happy. Beaming, graduation-gowned, with her new man. He wondered what their future together could have been, if he hadn't been greedy, and listened to her. An ex-con with a record for white-collar crime has time for regrets.

Karen Al-Ghabban is a lover of words and languages. Married, two children and two dogs.

Swallowing Stars

We lie on our backs, the August soil, and swallow the stars over the bay. Is this guy for real? Yes. Realer than anyone I'd known. His "side of the tracks" was ten times better because on his side, they sought the stars, earth, salt. Safety not first.

Elaina likes to write across genres while *The Golden Girls* play in the background. *elainawrites.com*

The Beginning of the End of the Line

As the train lurched back to movement, she tightened her grip on the railing, remaining upright despite being jostled. Nearby, a young man rose to offer his seat. Above, a sign read: Priority seating for elderly passengers. She glimpsed her reflection in the window. When had she begun to qualify?

Elizabeth Barton moves words around for fun and profit while living in Chicago with her husband, two cats, and more than a little self-doubt. *lizardesque.wordpress*

Permanent Scars

The holes in the glass remind her of gaping wounds. But there isn't any bleeding to staunch, nothing to stitch. Red lights flash outside her window, slashing the night with their urgency. Alerting all nearby that something bad happened here. She'd bear the ugly scars forever.

Philip Goldberg is an avid Pickleball player, Wordle lover, and a fiction writer with many stories published.

Wheels on My Cart

Mr. Juan Hernandez is friendly but possibly without friends. Never saw him with any.

He suffered a reversal in fortune, but, as his way, He didn't complain. Never does.

He was forced to leave behind everything he owned.

"Why?" I asked.

"Wheels on my shopping cart came off," he said.

Michael is a lawyer and a storyteller, or perhaps the other way around.

The 7:13

Shells crunch underfoot as you pound down the station stairs, reaching the platform in a huff. Loosening your tie, you steal a moment to catch your breath. Our eyes meet ... you smile. I smile back. Sparks fly. Where could the train take us tonight? Sliding doors close on our exchange.

Jass Aujla plans perfect (fictional) murders in between her day-job meetings. *jassaujla.com*

Unhappy Hour

I imbibed. My dull headache and baggy eyes proof of the proof from the evening before. These vice marks stare at me in the mirror. The morning marred, my work hours sluggish, and yet I welcome and dread the evening hours. Unhappy Hour. Am I an alcoholic?

Lillian Stulich is a weekday teacher and a weekend writer. *littleghostpublishing.com*

Watering the Lawn

My tears fell into the clover patch as I mowed. Cutting it was like giving a haircut to a young child, except there was no cut against the blade. The emerald-green tops fell over with purpose, settling into the soil to nurture what was left of its body.

John McCaffrey is an author, playwright, columnist, and creative writing teacher.

Like Breath

A lavender candle glows on the sill of our bedroom window. Beth used to keep the window open, just a crack, even in winter. I was never sure why. It slides open, wide. Whispers of night air ripple through the screen and catch the candle flame which flickers and dies.

Keith Hood is a writer and photographer who lives in Ann Arbor, MI.

Of Skills & Skillets

The skillet lived a bland life. Stocked and stacked. Tucked and trapped. Vacuum sealed. The basement its forever home. Alongside burners, boilers, and barbecues. Back-ups (bedframes and board books) fully baked. After twenty years consuming echoes, new plots long overdue. Eager to break wraps and exercise skills. Awaiting unexpected sizzle.

Jen Schneider is an educator who lives, writes, and works in small spaces throughout Pennsylvania.

Sky Defender

The little boy looks up at the heavens. He spies all the eerie animal shapes in the clouds and wonders if he could summon the most terrible creature among them to leap down from the sky and land on his older sister. Sis never knew what hit her.

Phillip Temples has published five mystery-thriller novels, a novella, and two short story anthologies in addition to over 180 short stories online. *temples.com*

Courting

The scream ended and the night was silent once more.

The next morning, one of the dog foxes had a cut above his eye and a split ear. The other had a large open wound on his back. Split Ear, the Victor, laid down in the sun, beside the vixen.

Peter Snell was a bookseller, and he wears a lot of red in December. Facebook *@bartons.bookshop*

Legacies

Out of the blue my son announces he wants to build something. I'm unsurprised.

One grandfather, a carpenter, filled our home with custom pieces. The other, a fellow engineer, constructed a backyard skating rink when I was little. Now I watch their DNA spiraling through time, from heart to fingertips.

Beth Manca's Aunt Jean has written a memoir and her cousin Barry is a young adult novelist.

Caught Out

She sneezed. Heart beating wildly, she tried to run, but it was useless. They were on her in seconds. "No, please," she cried as the frenzied attack began.

"It's only allergies." Those were her last words.

Natalie is an ex-military, non-conformist theologian in training who regularly scribbles poetry and snippets of stories on any paper she can salvage from her handbag.

Secret Flight

Secret flight, crew takes a military intel guy to Israel. Landed, two vans arrive. One takes the spook away. The other takes the crew--thru security gates--no passport control! On city streets, they arrive at a hotel/restaurant complex. " Stay here tonight--do not leave. You're not really here.

Pete Obermanns is a retired Navy helicopter pilot, a big fan of sci-fi, and SpaceX and lives in Germany.

Teeth

Waking up is like a kick in the teeth. I'll wash my face with the blood in the bathroom sink, powder my nose with the crushed-up bones, and smile with nothing but gum. Wonder when the tooth fairy will say that it's all too much.

Casey DaBreo expresses herself through whatever means necessary and reads a lot of comic books. *caseydabreo.myportfolio.com*

In the Cards

Two Aces, two eights; the Deadman's Hand. Sam remained stony. Two players left. Winner and loser. Pete's pinkie twitched. Sam bluffed. Success! A smirk covered relief when he reached for the pot. Stepping out into a dawn light felt like cheating the grim reaper. Sam never knew what hit him.

Rosie Cullen lives in Manchester, UK, and likes writing all kinds of little stuff but still loves her big novel *The Lucky Country* best. *mcullenauthor.wordpress.com*

Missing

An African American female, age twelve, last seen on Riverside Avenue at 2:30 pm wearing a pink jacket with a unicorn on its hood. A third false sighting. Parents' lives paused. A school picture of the happy, smiling sixth grader. No search parties. No media coverage. No one knows she's gone.

Azizat Danmole is an Illinois-hearted Missourian who writes, instructs writing, and counsels young people. Facebook *@adanmole*

Glitter-less Christmas

"It's garish," Grandmother said with a frown, removing my ornament from her perfect tree. Mama had loved that ornament—a salt-dough disc with my thumbprint and lots of glitter. Christmas would be different this year. A tree from a magazine cover but lacking any heart. I miss her.

Melissa Miles is a children's book author, certified educator, registered nurse, and board chair of Superhero Success Foundation, Inc. Twitter *@melissajmiles*

Methamphetamine or C10H15N

Produce, deal, don't sample! The chemist's mantra replays mindlessly, blending the illegal concoction, quick money, zombie-like junkies plentiful. Cognizant his hyper-sensitive skin crawls, light becomes painful, paranoia consuming. The delivery gal enters the jarred door to discover his slit wrists. Sadly, she never delivered; he never called again.

Deb Obermanns is an avid traveler, lover of storytelling, and international school teacher.

Sludge Cakes

Once I stood in the vibrant center. I took or rejected what came to me from my left and right. But the center became a centrifuge, flinging both sides to their ends, leaving sludge cakes filled with the blinding smoke of lies. Now in the lonely center, I stand bewildered.

Steve Bailey lives in Richmond, Virginia, where he remains bewildered.

Life's Rhythm

She argues with her husband about taking down the tree: he wants it cut to the ground; she wants eight feet remaining. She wins. The fungi move in first. Then insects—so many insects. Finally pileated woodpeckers arrive; she arches her eyebrow smugly his way, enjoying the beautiful staccato rhythm.

By day, Kathryn teaches; by night, she resurrects gods, goddesses, folk, and fairy tales. Twitter *@katecanwrite*

Waiting to Inhale

I see only water all around. I need to breathe, yet there's no panic.

Am I drowning? Go ahead and breathe. Amazingly, only air rushes in. Through my jumbled senses I hear my name. Looking up, I see your face.

"Are you OK?"

"Whoa, that is some SPICY salsa."

Deborah Jones is a word game devotee who aims to get Wordle on the first try. She also plans to win the lottery.

Commitment

"We're asking you all to bear with us this afternoon," announced Rob's red-faced office manager.

Rob shrugged, while suspecting his expectation was illegal. An hour later, he trotted to the utility room, filled a plastic bucket with tap water, and headed for one of the non-flushing toilets.

Tim Dadswell is a retired civil servant, who loves the countryside and writing short fiction. Twitter *@timd_writer*

The Wedding

I hadn't heard from my son in over a year. His call came late one night. I was ecstatic! Asking him how he was, he said he'd been seeing a therapist, he was getting married,

I wasn't invited. My hand clinched my chest, heartache took me to my knees.

Ami is an author and poet, living in Southport, NC. *gypsieswritingmusingsquotes-gripes.wordpress.com*

Misspelling

The spell called for moonfish, but tuna would have to do—supply chain issues. She stirred it into the cauldron while reciting the incantation and picturing her beloved becoming warm again, suffused with life, coming to embrace her.

She waited. Her withering jade plant revived to a vibrant green.

Elizabeth Barton moves words around for fun and profit while living in Chicago with her husband, two cats, and more than a little self-doubt. *lizardesque.wordpress.com*

I Am a Rock

It was easier to call himself a widower and build a wall of books. Widower had a certain verve. A lack of fault. When he deigned to have company, he invented new, creative deaths for Claire. Train crash. Cancer. Of course, in books he still couldn't escape the word "cuckolded."

Yash Seyedbagheri's work has been published in SmokeLong Quarterly, The Journal of Compressed Creative Arts, Write City Magazine, and Ariel Chart, among others.

Faerie Food

"Swat it!" screamed Evie.

Fiona whooshed the fae-swatter through the air and missed. She whooshed again. Another miss. The angry creature darted at her, translucent wings glimmering in the firelight. Whoosh and whomp! Glitter rained as the faerie hurled across the cave. Evie opened her mouth to scream but swallowed.

Rita Riebel Mitchell writes at home in South Jersey where she lives in the forest and believes in faeries. Find her on Twitter @rita_jr

Untitled Country Song

Lost my job at the Bump and Brew.

Boss said, "Elmer, it's quits for you.

Lost my truck when the brakes broke free. Flying down the highway at ninety-three.

Lost my mind when I lost my dear. Guess it's time to drink another beer? pack my fishing gear? jump off a pier?

Ann S. Epstein, whose height in inches is roughly commensurate with this story's length in words, writes fiction and memoir. *asewovenwords.com*

Golden Years

She's all business this morning with her 8:00 am report. 152/90 not bad, I say, hoping to calm her. I wonder when we last danced. We used to go places. Can it be the years that aged us? Our dreams to old to reach; it's all prayers now.

Pasquale Trozzolo is a retired madman from Kansas. He and his wife Joan still dance and stuff and enjoy acting like seventy is the new fifty. Facebook *@poetpasquale*

Kyiv 2032

A small patch of sunflowers protected by a white fence and a park ranger swayed grandly behind a historical marker. The mother pointed excitedly while three small heads turned in awe. "This is where the Russian soldier died with a pocketful of seeds. Your babusya would be so proud."

Teri M. Brown, debut author of *Sunflowers Beneath the Snow*, connects readers to characters they'd love to invite to lunch.

Ornithology

Stupidly, when I was out bird watching, I left my wellies behind in the car when I went for a walk beside the lake. The spring flowers were abundant; but unfortunately, so were the vicious stinging nettles. Now my knees are really humming. Does anyone have any sound-proof trousers?

Peter Snell was a bookseller, and he wears a lot of red in December. Facebook *@bartons.bookshop*

Baby at 44

Middle-aged eyes intertwine against a playground heart, squinting through fuzzy blossom moonlight. Desperately engaged, mesmerized by the beauty of surprise baby's crescent cheeks, pouting lips. Mama-made four times, bitter towards the cruelty of time, clinging to this rocking chair moment: impossible wishfulness that babies could forever keep.

Jade Visone writes with soul-filled honesty about the struggles and magic of mothering, love, life, dandelions, and stars. Instagram *@mrsvisoney*

Devourer

I feel its presence behind me. I try to work but fail. Rage fills me. I turn and grab it. I smash it against the wall again and again, then hurl it away. Time passes. One biscuit fragment has fallen near my feet. I eat it, crying. I never win.

Dom is a game designer, programmer, artist and writer who lives in London, UK.

Tomorrow, or Perhaps the Next Day

Something dreadful was bound to strike. With all the turmoil and rage and waves of discontent circling the city, how could it not? But instead of doom she found a lilac in bloom, felt the morning sun and a cool breeze on her skin. Sometimes it happens: a beautiful day!

Chuck Augello is the author of *The Revolving Heart*, a Best Books of 2020 selection by Kirkus Reviews. *cda.thedailyvonnegut.com*

My Hero

John panned his video camera from the upper rapids to the brink of Niagara Falls.

Running, he ditched his camera and gave his baby boy to his wife. A hero to me and all, he plucked a seventeen-year-old girl from the whitewater, twenty-five feet from the brink.

Cooking, quilting, knitting, and occasionally writing, keep Rose busy and off the streets.

Changing With the Times

They were a tight-knit group, friends for decades despite wide variations in political views. The agreement to avoid certain conversation topics was key. Some years back, this became increasingly difficult during their monthly card games. Thus, they instituted a new rule: no more games that involve trump cards.

Elizabeth Barton is a writer/editor living in Chicago with her husband, two cats, and more than a little self-doubt. *lizardesque.wordpress*

Tiny World

An early morning walk has my eyes falling upon a spider's web decorated with dewdrops that sparkle in the rising sun. This spider must have had a busy night, spinning and preparing her net for the next meal. I see it now; her dinner awaits, wrapped within the delicate strands.

Kim Lengling drops nuggets of hope as an author, podcast host, and TV Show Host. *kimlenglingauthor.com*

Crooked

Crooked, as usual, he rushed to straighten his tie before the woman of his dreams strolled through his front door. Tying ties had never been his forte. Over the years, Charlie had accepted the crooked Windsor knot as his signature style. Hopefully, she would do the same.

Emily Holewcynski is a mom of five, writer, and professional shoe-tier/sandwich-maker/boogeyman-catcher.

Stick in the Mud

Archie loved splashing in puddles.

"Watch out for the Mud Monster!" his grandpop yelled.

'Silly grandpop.'

Archie ran ahead and stomped through a yummy puddle; so deep and squelchy. He jumped in the middle. What a great muddy splash! Then his wellies were stuck—and it was too late.

Rosie Cullen lives in Manchester, UK, and likes writing all kinds of little stuff but still loves her big novel *The Lucky Country* best. *rmcullenauthor.wordpress.com*

Settlement

Sleep eluded her. Frank's periods of apnea lasted as long as thirty seconds, allowing Stella to listen to the ancient house creaking, in response to imperceptible shifts of earth beneath it. But I won't settle, she decided. I will leave tomorrow. She closed her eyes and drifted off to sleep.

Deborah Jones is a retired TV news writer/producer with a passion for red wine, wombats, and Oxford commas—not necessarily in that order.

Evil Undetected

The spring I turned seventeen, a heat wave swallowed my home-town. Scorching days decomposed the murdered girls' bodies so fast, evidence incinerated like tinder tossed onto a bonfire. I'd thought evil would be easy to spot, detonating an internal alarm if I looked into its eyes. I'd been dead wrong.

Melissa Miles is a children's book author, certified educator, registered nurse, and board chair of Superhero Success Foundation, Inc. Twitter *@melissajmiles*

The Vasa

A common sailor boards his ship, climbs the mast and leaves Stock-holm harbor with a slight breeze. Suddenly, a gust tips the top-heavy ship over. Open gun-ports take in water, the ship floods. He jumps from the mast, and lives. The Vasa sinks—there to stay for hundreds of years.

Pete Obermanns is a retired Navy helicopter pilot, a big fan of sci-fi, and SpaceX and lives in Germany.

Europacar, Agip, and Euroass

Political science doctor, eyeglasses, scarf, umbrella consistently. One trip to Italy and from his cerebral world he declares:

"The only country where U-rope- a- car, buying gas is A- gyp, and when there is an accident it is Your-ass." A deadening silence fills the car, followed by decades of laughter.

Deb Obermanns is an avid traveler, lover of storytelling, and international school teacher.

Measured

Food had always provided a measure of control in the storm of her life. She scoured ingredient lists for artificial something or other. She shopped organic. Food was routine, comfort. Now, meals were measured teaspoon by teaspoon. When food lost its taste, she measured her life in breaths.

A special education teacher by day, Theresa Milstein writes middle grade, YA, and dabbles in poetry. *theresamilstein.blogspot.com*

Words Count

Alan slowly counted the number of words. 374. David had led a narrow life, padded out to 374 words by an anonymous obituary writer. Since Mary had died, Alan had been counting; a word league. Mary had received 287. The world's most wonderful wife, not even in the top division.

John Holmes is a writer who cycles or a cyclist who writes.

Irretrievable

"You both agree the marriage is irretrievably broken?" The judge's words hit my ears like a sonic boom, echoing like a coin dully ricocheting off the walls of an empty well. But could it be irretrievable if it was never even right to begin with?

I somehow manage a "yes."

Ashley Emert is a pop culture-loving word nerd who also happens to be a bit of a cat lady.

Rock On

Heavy bass leaked from the stranger's headphones, filling the space between them.

"Nice music," he said, thinking she'd take the clue and turn it down. She did not. Slowly they began to bounce their heads to the rhythm. Theirs was a relationship forged by the beat of a discrepant drummer.

Mary Boone lives in Tacoma, WA, where she writes nonfiction books for children. *boonewrites.com*

Classics

She looked like herself more than other days—pink watercolor cheeks, glossy skin, razor cheekbones. Even her voice quaked with a rhythm, "I'll have a house coffee with soy, thanks." It's not like she'd gone for a run or done any writing. Blame the Dr Martens who steered the sway.

Elaina likes to write across genres while *The Golden Girls* play in the background. *elainawrites.com*

The Date

"Here, dear. Look what I found."

I gingerly took the date-inscribed photo from my grandmother, immediately recognizing the covered face and white dress.

"How sweet were you for your First Communion?" she says, her eyes beaming with pride. I didn't have the heart to tell her. 10/31/1992.

Elizabeth Lorayne is a printmaker, artist, and award-winning author on the Northshore of Massachusetts. *elizabethlorayne.com*

The Dowager's Bodkin

Branwell's surprise was induced as much by the dowager's prowess with a blade as from seeing the gem-studded bodkin protruding from his chest. Though he had searched a lifetime for the priceless dagger, his final thought was that the widow was remarkably agile, despite having been dead for centuries.

Tim Canny is a writer in the dust of middle age specializing in children's stories characterized by a misguided sense of whimsy. Twitter *@tcanny*

Be Careful When You Help

He was sitting in the shade with his head in his hands.

"Dave, what's the matter?"

"I've lost my job."

"What?"

"I got some vape kits for a kid. «

Peter Snell was a bookseller, and he wears a lot of red in December. Facebook *@bartons.bookshop*

Progression

✓ Stroller

✓ Little Tykes

✓ Training wheels

✓ 10-speed

✓ Hot rod

✓ Mini Van

✓ Hybrid sedan

✓ Cadillac

✓ Uber

✓ Sunny Valley Retirement fun bus

I lower my paper as the hearse pulls up and quickly check my pulse.
Satisfied, I resume reading the obits.

Teri M. Brown, debut author of *Sunflowers Beneath the Snow*, connects readers to
characters they'd love to invite to lunch. *terimbrown.com*

On The Spectrum

Who is that handsome guy at the bar? he heard her ask.

Oh, that's Daniel, nice guy, masters' prepared, but the rumor is he's on the spectrum. Years of conversion therapy to make an autistic person normal, left scars. He downed his beer, ordered a second and studied his wrists.

Patricia Pollack is a nurse educator, avid traveler, and proud mother.

Death Bed Wishes

Mike, brain shriveled, Ph.D with a loving family. Always said, "No one on their deathbed wishes they had spent more time at the office."

I held his hand. He opened his eyes and with a sparkle he passed to the other side. I wish I had gone too.

Domini Boling recently moved to the coast where she watches the waves and remembers things.

We Made it Through Winter

We made it through winter, but not without scar. Every gosling waddling in single file reminds us that we survived. But this year is different. Our scars are a sign that we are stronger; though hidden internally and escaping only after a third neat Belvedere they are no less real.

Terrence Litwiller is grateful for his fun and adventures with his grandson Liam. *terrencelitwiller.com*

Surrender

"Let's wait a couple days," the doctor says. Instead, I stare into the static screen breathless and sinking. Longing to re-ignite the tiny flicker of life that danced among the shadows. Rational me knows when to admit defeat, to forgive my heart's surrender. I wake up to red.

Catie Daly is a New Jersey mom of four who loves reading, writing, and nachos. *catiedalywrites.com*

Near Bedtime ... or, Cookie Dough

Little Ed sat at the kitchen table, finishing the last of his chocolate milk. His mother, Alice, dug into the bottom of an ice cream container with her spoon.

— Little Ed: Is that cookie dough ice cream?

— His mother: No it's not.

— Little Ed: Then what's the point? ...

David Sydney is a physician from Newtown, PA.

Dear Diary

Last week, we met. In my diary, I downplayed the whole event to protect myself. But looking back on that entry, I realize now that the lack of description says so much more than if I had catalogued every blink and smile. It was important, but I was a chicken.

Emily Holeczynski is a mom of five, writer, and professional shoe-tier/sandwich-maker/boogeyman-catcher.

Hitler's Eagles Nest

Standing upon Hitler's Eagles Nest in Bavaria—one looks down over an expansive view. Many tall, beautiful mountains. Valleys, with rivers, even lakes within them. Green foliage everywhere. Far below, a single tour boat plies its way up the narrow Königsee Lake to Saint Bartholomew's Church. Peace has supplanted evil.

Pete Obermanns is a retired Navy helicopter pilot, a big fan of sci-fi, and SpaceX and lives in Germany.

Thanks for Nothing

And with that kiss, Snow White opened her eyes, and gazed upon the handsome prince that broke the witch's spell. She was captivated by his thick locks, and deep, dark eyes. His features were strong, and his jaw square. "Whoa! What's that on your lip?"

E. O'Neill, who wants to write *Catcher in the Rye,* has authored two well-received customer reviews on Amazon.

The Rest

Mum moved into a care home today. She doesn't care and it isn't home. Family visitors will be greeted as strangers. Friends will send cards that are difficult to open, impossible to read. Tonight, head on the new pillow, she will be at rest. The rest of her life.

Geja Hadderingh is a reluctant writer who loves to edit.

Highest Form of Flattery

She panicked when their toddler audibly struggled to bend over. It had happened before. She picked up the phone to call the pediatrician but stopped when her worried husband dropped his keys. "Honey," she said as he moaned, retrieving them from the floor. "She thinks that's just how it's done!"

Deborah Jones is a retired TV news writer/producer with a passion for wombats, red wine, and Oxford commas—not necessarily in that order.

Sisters

They were a team, taking turns calling their increasingly frail and stubborn mother. After the fall, one drove her to appointments while the other managed bills. After the dementia diagnosis, one cleaned out a forty-year home while the other found a new one. It was always too much and never enough.

A special education teacher by day, Theresa Milstein writes middle grade, YA, and dabbles in poetry. *theresamilstein.blogspot.com*

A Conversation

"A plane's crashed," she said.

Into the World Trade Center, she quivered.
What are you talking about?

"Your husband," she declared, and I saw she was crying.

Oh, he's fine. He's downstairs.

I didn't know what she was talking about.

But the world had just changed.

Alison Davidson is a Brit living in New Jersey with a passion for dogs, hiking, and now writing.

Bomb Threat

Inside a toilet cubicle, phone in hand, he squirmed on his white oval perch.

"I can't stay in here--my manager will miss me," he protested. "It's probably a hoax."

He listened.

"Flying glass? Oh yeah, I guess. Alright, I will. Yes, I promise. Don't worry, Ma."

Tim Dadswell is a retired civil servant, who loves the countryside and writing short fiction. Twitter *@timd_writer*

Restless

I've been restless before, but not for a while and not like this. I should feel weighty, but I'm elated, passionate, excited. Uncharacteristically, I want to go for a run. That is categorically NOT what I want to do. Tender. Smooth. Your hand, my thigh. It's decided ... Let's go.

Laura Cooney lives in Edinburgh, UK and mainly writes children's fiction.

Twelve

"TWELVE!" she screamed, compelling him to run upstairs.

"Twelve what?" he panted through the doorway.

She turned, brandishing her deodorant.

"Twelve turns to get it working, brand new."

"That's it?" he asked.

"It's a big deal," she answered.

"I have finally answered the question, 'What is wrong with this world?'"

Emmy-award-winner Amy Bass is a writer, Manhattanville College professor, and sport thinker. *amybass.net*

A Shadow's Dance

Standing on her porch on a winter's moonlit night, the woman appreciates the beauty of the stillness. Shadows enter the yard, dancing and swaying to a silent tune. Then, one shadow shifts, taking on a menacing form. In a whisper, the shadow speaks to the woman of her nightmares.

Kim Lengling is an author and likes to chat with the critters that reside in her Realm. *kimlenglingauthor.com*

In Transit

She played post punk bass, eyes laughing from the joy of random encounter. An old flame, she explained, waiting for the train. Now we sat motionless in transit, a suicide on the tracks. The voice told us to evacuate. We parted from the aimless crowd, us for a taxi they to the bar.

Jenny Dunbar continues to make ceramics and haikus in these strange times.

When Your Girl Has Left You

Clyde takes aim at the shit stain with his piss. Try as he might, he cannot dislodge the hardened fecal matter on the side of the rim. He yells for Julie to come clean the toilet bowl. His command is met with a deafening silence.

Phillip Temples, of Watertown, Massachusetts, has published five mystery-thriller novels, a novella, and two short story anthologies. *temples.com*

Fragile

He is as fragile as the fresh mown grass, cut and scattered, spreading juices for a short time, then drying and blowing away, bereft of perfume. He counts the springs to come. Antonio breathes deeply, inhales the essence of green into his being, to assuage the ache of mortality.

Lou Giansante works with words and sounds, often together.

I Saved a Life Today

A tiny baby gecko, pale pink like a fetus was lounging in my sink. I grabbed a plastic cup. She saw my shadow and darted madly. But I was quicker. I captured her. Stunned, she stood motionless. I brought her outside and watched her run boldly, into the world's immensity.

Janet Hiller loves reading poetry and writing about moments of wonder that she witnesses daily.

Love at First Sight

John fell in love at first sight with the star of the local bordello, fell to his knees, and proposed. She accepted but refused to have sex with him. A traditionalist, she wanted to wait till her wedding night to be disappointed.

Michael Fryd, a retired scientist, is now writing in Philadelphia.

Name Change

Today, she called me by the wrong name.

"Paul." Her husband's name. She didn't notice her mistake and I wasn't going to tell her. Paul died eight years ago. It's good that he's still remembered; that she has found someone new to love, as much as she had loved him.

John Holmes is a writer who likes to cycle.

They Tried

After losing 27 to 0, Coach Fromberg addressed the Little Leaguers:

— Coach: 27 runs …
— Louie: I got on base.
— Coach: True, Louie … Our only runner, and you were hit by a pitch.
— Several players: We tried, Coach Fromberg.
— Coach: Very true … But trying's not what it used to be.

David Sydney is a physician from Newtown, PA.

Classroom

I need to know whether they're painting this room. Taking everything down will be no small feat. Photos, posters, maps, flags, bookcases, window breakers, CPR valves, and toys. Each item a heavy testament, sweat poured out for lessons passed. Memorials to days we survived. We either learn, or we don't.

Tiffany Hendrix is a friendly neighborhood language teacher in western Colorado. *originalgeotrix.wordpress*

The Tie that Binds

That's it! It's over! I've had enough. Nothing I do is right, you criticize everything, you put me down, you embarrass me in front of the kids. I can't take it anymore. We're done. Finito! Silence. Right. That's it then. They stare at each other.

Same time next week, Mum?

Ellen Fox is an award-winning playwright, who has also written for radio, film, and television.

On Drying Out

He ceased writing, approached the dryer, and removed the fitted sheet. He dislodged four soggy recalcitrant T-shirts that had found their way to the sheet's elasticized corners. Threw the mess back into the dryer. Fifteen minutes later the T-shirts of despair had found their way back to the corners; very much enjoying their "fuck you" moment.

Steve Zettler is the author of *Careless Love* and *Piece of Cake* (2023).

Smokestack

No grave markers exist. Nor any small stones that would lie atop them. Still, people tread the paths aware of what's under their feet. Somber, silent on such a sunny day, until they come upon a smokestack, long extinguished from belching ash gray fog around the clock.

Philip love doing Wordle, playing Pickleball, and writing short fiction, many of which have made it into magazines.

Flashing

The first time, in the privacy of her bedroom, she stripped down to her undies.

Second time, she whipped her sheets off in a frenzy. Another time, she rubbed ice to cool the burning heat. Gazing at her lover, she fanned her glistening skin. Couldn't take it anymore. Hot flashes.

A special education teacher by day, Theresa Milstein writes middle grade, YA, and dabbles in poetry. *theresamilstein.blogspot.com*

Thyestes Thinks of Dining Out

After a violent, mythic life, in which a rival had tricked him into eating his slaughtered children, exiled Greek king Thyestes was hungry for comfort and peace. His brother recommended a special restaurant. "They'll serve you like you're family there."

"That," Thyestes replied, "is what I'm afraid of."

Joel Savishinsky's *Breaking the Watch: The Meanings of Retirement in America*, won the Gerontology Society's book-of-the-year prize. Ithaca.edu *@savishin*

Brush and Pen

He illustrates, she writes. Designing a delicately balanced world masked with paint and pen strokes. He loves the earth and she the sky. Stoically, confronting the future equipped with distinctive tools: linen canvas and brushes, watermark paper and quill. Braving adversity they recreate a unique reality that eradicates intellectual anarchy.

Deb Obermanns is an avid traveler, lover of storytelling, and international school teacher.

A Contrast of Evil Versus Good

Violence, destruction, death, fear and trauma in every heart. Ukraine. A mother and two daughters fled Kiev, arrived by train in Germany. There they were treated with love, hugs and tenderness. Safety, stability and friendship. Free housing, clothing, food, bicycles, job offers, education. The Devil's handiwork versus God's love.

Pete Obermanns is a retired Navy helicopter pilot, a big fan of sci-fi and SpaceX, and lives in Germany.

Drinking Al Fresco

There's a fly in my wine, but I'll drink it anyway. Lazing on my swing seat, contemplating life, dogs at my feet, I pick up my glass and gaze into the golden nectar. There are now three flies swimming, getting gamely drunk. I sigh. It's been a long week.

Alison Davidson is a Brit living in New Jersey with a passion for dogs, hiking, and now writing.

Curling Iron

My anthem to my non-verbal daughter shuffled onto Spotify, silent joyful tears tumbled. I curled her teenage hair, as she asked, for the first time in her life. Awakening slowly: her terms, from silence and insecurities. Beauty stole my breath.

She mumbled, "No pictures, mommy, I probably look stupid."

Jade Visone writes with soul-filled honesty about the struggles and magic of mothering, love, life, dandelions, and stars.

The Great Escape

Downright oppressive. Push the mattress through the window. It's time to set up camp on the wrought-iron balcony hanging over an asphalt desert. Jukebox wails whenever the door of Teddy's Lounge swings open.

"Somebody shut that dog up!" It's not a fire I need to escape. Just the heat.

E. O'Neill doesn't sleep on a fire escape, but pumps quarters into the jukebox at Teddy's Lounge at an alarming rate.

Connections

She wheeled her vacuum cleaner into the windowless basement room. Warbling an uplifting song, she removed a plug from the one and only socket. Oblivious to a fading electrical hum, she plugged in her machine and started work. Valuable data languished inside the newly installed processing device.

Tim Dadswell is a retired civil servant, who loves the countryside and writing short fiction. Twitter: *@timd_writer*

What's in There?

"Something to play with," his father answers.

"Basketball?" the boy guesses. Dad chuckles. Goes back to the game on TV.

"Something sweet," his mother replies.

"Watermelon?" the child ventures.

Mom shakes her head. Yawns. Naps.

"Bomb!" the boy decides. When that bulge explodes, it will blow up his family forever.

At five feet give or take, Ann S. Epstein is a fan of short, but she also likes long stories, stemmed roses, and summer days.

Change is a Process

I settled onto the snowy mountain. Smoke escaped my nostrils as I exhaled a cleansing breath. My tail tucked under me; my wings folded. I will not eat humans nor set cities ablaze—my mantra interrupted as my scales deflected a human's arrows. He was delicious. Change is a process.

Katie is not, nor does she have a dragon, but she does have three large, adopted mutts who could be described as having dragon's breath. *authorkatiehizen.com*

Taking Shelter

Our family never could agree where we'd hide when the tornado came. My vote was for grandpa's fallout shelter next to the barn. But I was 'just a kid,' dad was claustrophobic, and Grammie Lynn wheelchair bound. They opted for the basement. I figured living with guilt was still living.

Chet Ensign takes shelter in northern New Jersey.

Jubilee Day

The sound of canon fire ricochets around Hyde Park. Bodies do not fall in the sunshine. Instead, as one, the jubilant throng walks The Mall in celebration of seventy years of dedication and duty. A woman, leaning on a cane, waves from the balcony of her home. My Queen.

Apple Gidley, currently living in the Caribbean, is a global nomad who writes historical fiction, essays, and more. *applegidley.com*

Scar

Skin pulled tight, lines and shading etched into the skin, the artist's hands create deft beauty around the scar, once a source of revulsion and dismay, now a symbol of strength and triumph. A ring of yellow roses sparkle. It's not a cover-up; it's a spotlight, a focus, a liberation.

Annalisa Crawford writes with her canine muse warming her feet and a giant mug of tea in her hand. linktr.ee *@annalisa_crawford*

Baby Boy

Her theory of parenting: keep him alive. Keep the monsters at bay and always love him enough. So he could leave. That was the goal. She accepted it. Parents who didn't were crazy. Whining about the day the nest would be empty while it was still full to the brim.

Janet Clare lives and works and worries in Los Angeles.

Gift for the Givers

We were explicit: we did not want a microwave. So, his family gave us one for Christmas. I told my mother about it on the phone. Later, when we opened gifts at my parents' house, she held aloft a mink coat from my father. "Oh, look!" she exclaimed, "a microwave!"

Deborah Jones is a retired TV news writer/producer with a passion for wombats, red wine, and Oxford commas—not necessarily in that order.

Watermelon

When I ask about watermelons, the grey-haired grocer looks over the mound, sniffs for traces of earth where they once laid, heavy with water. He thumps, holds one up and whispers there's a deep ring to ripeness. I lean to listen; sun faded rind still warm against my ear.

Karen's in love with words, folklore, and the grain of tree bark and waves of color in her assemblage art. *karenpiercegonzalez.blogspot.com*

Newly Refurbished Basement

"Night Fever" plays on my father's old stereo. We sit in a boy/girl/boy/girl circle. I spin an empty 7-Up bottle. Land on Mike Green, my Hebrew-school crush. Friends with Farah Fawcett layers and budding breasts titter. Mike opens closet. We enter blackness. "Want to kiss?" he asks. I scram.

Jen Lang is a California transplant in Tel Aviv, whose prize-winning essays appear in various journals and whose memoir *Places We Left Behind*, will be published by Vine Leaves Press, 2023. Facebook *@israelwritersstudio*

Ned's 95th

A number of Ned's relatives celebrated Ned's 95th with him ...

Happy birthday, Uncle Ned.

What?

Happy birthday, Grampa.

Huh?

I'm Frank, remember me?

What?

Uncle Ned, you made it to ninety-five ...

Huh?

I've never you seen you so good ...

David Sydney is a physician from Newtown, PA.

Bingo

All he had left to do was book a one-way to Portland, then shave his head at the airport. He folded the winning lottery ticket into his pocket.

"Cleveland conference again?" asked his wife when she saw the suitcase. He grabbed it and kissed her.

"What a good guess."

Shoshauna Shy enjoys being with trees, books, cats, chocolate, and her husband, preferably all at the same time.

Another Monday Morning

Am I doing it wrong? Is there a chef's secret I'm not aware of? Please Lord, give me patience, if not guidance. Show me the way. I'm not looking to break any laws of Newton or Murphy. I just want to understand them and know why it's always jelly-side down!

E. O'Neill has conquered the "jelly-side down" problem—he uses butter now.

Tempest

The green sky sucks up the air. Spits it out in furious, twisting wind. Trees bend in reverence. Animals scurry in fear. Flash, boom, the ground trembles. Clouds rupture. Rain rushes down in torrents, smacking all in its path. It's the end of the world. Again.

Phil Goldberg is an avid Pickleball player, Wordle lover, and a fiction writer with many stories published.

The Last Goodbye

Flying halfway around the world, to see my mother one last time. In the wee hours of the morning, she opened her eyes, squeezed my hand. Took her last breath. Echoing the koel, the uwu bird's plaintive cry, "Kowel, kowel," I'm here.

Trying to reach her on the other side.

Kwan Kew Lai is an author, a Harvard medical faculty physician, an infectious disease specialist, a disaster response volunteer, an artist, and a runner. *kwankewlai.com*

Cheeky Lad

The puerile adolescent is always talking shit! Nothing is spared. Today, he fixates on "buns". Cinnamon, honey, Scottish baps ... even his mother's hot cross buns! His sexual innuendos aren't unnoticed or appreciated. Judging by his slight build and braggadocio monologue he has never savored a single tempting bite!

Deb Obermanns is an avid traveler, lover of storytelling, and international school teacher.

Skitter, Skatter

Skitter, Scatter, Pitter Patter. The nightmare came closer. Sniffing and crawling, the black orbs stared in unfocused horror. Drawing near, I leapt, ascending to the heavens in desperate hope. Closer it came, winding and searching, nothing would stop it. A plea escaped my lungs. "Richard. It's a rat!"

Damien is passionate about writing and reimagining the lost era of pulp fiction. His works centers on the creepy and the macabre.

Choices

My grief complicated. I swore I saw her fishing off the pier one summer. Another year I saw her walking down a city street. Years earlier at fifty-one years old, the alcohol, and antidepressants had taken her out. She chose her own destiny every day. I chose to watch.

Domini Boling recently moved to the coast where she watches the waves and remembers things.

Vital Signs

As a new faculty member during Vietnam, I'd lost my student deferment. Frantic, I brought the dean a blood pressure cuff and stethoscope, requesting he write my draft board about how important I was. He cursorily examined me, said don't worry: I'll write that the college considers you absolutely vital.

Joel Savishinsky, author of *Breaking the Watch: The Meanings of Retirement in America*, continues to believe in the value of letters. Ithaca.edu @savishin

Independence Day

The sudden glow in a darkened sky illuminates the outline of a cityscape. A flash of light displays trees shivering on the horizon. Bombs bursting in air reveal the silhouette of a tattered flag. A warm, summer night in Ukraine as citizens and soldiers die for freedom.

Teri M. Brown, debut author of *Sunflowers Beneath the Snow*, connects readers to characters they'd love to invite to lunch. *terimbrown.com*

Shooting Star

Initially you showed up as a shooting star, bolting out of the black and into the blue. Once again you entered my world, this time desperate, fizzling and fading. I wish upon a star that you may discover who you are. Fallen star, your universe is too small.

Paul Hertig has spent his life under the stars, walking the road of experiential learning. Apu.edu @*phertig*

In Dresden

Werner threads his way down a narrow, energetic street, Miles Davis wafting over the crowd like weed smoke; the ironic window sign of the anachronistic, shoebox music shop responsible says 'Jazz is Dead.' *Even its afterlife is more exciting than his routine*, he thinks; time for a change.

Alastair Millar is an archaeologist by training and a translator by trade; he lives in the Czech Republic. *linktr.ee/alastairmillar*

Things That Are Breakable

My grandmother's sisters gave her glass headed dolls whose ownership they'd fought over for fifty years. Grandma made them calico dresses, attached plastic hands to their empty arms and packed them away. They've shared the same shoebox for nearly a century now, as quiet as the day they arrived.

Joanne Nelson is the keeper of many unlabeled shoe boxes. She is the author of *This Is How We Leave* and the forthcoming, *My Neglected Gods* (2023). *wakeupthewriterwithin.com*

Accidentally

Her neighbor says, "Don't wait for him to kill you. Leave now."

A year passes. A baby girl arrives.

"I accidentally bumped into a door (wall, chair)," she tells friends.

Another year passes.

He slams the child's foot in a door. "An accident," he says.

She "accidentally" packs, takes her daughter. Now she leaves.

Ann S. Epstein, whose height in inches is roughly commensurate with this story's length in words, writes fiction and memoir. *asewovenwords.com*

Youth Trip to Israel

We cram into one room, draping heads over bellies and hips, hands over legs and lips. Joey kisses and caresses Amy, Eric kiss-caresses me, Marcia kiss-caresses Craig, Craig kiss-caresses Joey, a carousel of hungry bodies galloping like horses, The Human League lyrics humming "Don't You Want Me?" in my ears.

Jen Lang is a California transplant in Tel Aviv, whose prize-winning essays appear in various journals and whose memoir *Places We Left Behind*, will be published by Vine Leaves Press, 2023. Facebook *@israelwritersstudio*

At Breakfast

He looked at his cup of coffee, then at his bowl of cereal. He studied his low bank statement, reflecting the most recent alimony payment. He looked at his dog, waiting for its breakfast. Was this truly man's best friend?

David Sydney is a physician from Newtown, PA.

Tap Shoes

Sweet sixteen draped disappointment and frustration. Those extra curves didn't match Instagram's skinny-girl standards. Oversized hoodies: fleece shields in mid-August heat, disguised insecurities. Dusk was her cue. She slipped on tap shoes: freedom, music, dance. She stomped songs of confidence with metal toes and moonlight.

Jade Visone writes with soul-filled honesty about the struggles and magic of mothering, love, life, dandelions, and stars.

Downstream

After the flood which washed away the walls and bridges and cars, I wished we could share the vibrancy of the new day, the clarity of the azure sky, the freshness of the air, the way neighbors emerge from their houses to offer aid. But you were miles downstream by then, misplaced.

Annalisa Crawford writes with her canine muse warming her feet and a giant mug of tea in her hand. linktr.ee @annalisa_crawford

A Night Unconvinced of Morning

The catch in your breath. Your cry in a language I don't know. Your limbs small swim through ever-fading shades of gray. The sudden surrender to a deeper sleep. Your wake-up call is a cold sweat. In the morning, a coffee cup rattles its saucer.

Cheryl Snell's books include poetry collections and the series of novels called *Bombay Trilogy*. Facebook *@cheryl.snell*

Another Win

I sternly presented several reasons for defunding the police as not liberal but sensible, correct and just. My father-in-law bowed his head and gave his law professor's validation to my argument. He didn't even mind that it was reductive. He agreed. Another imaginary argument won, eighth one today.

TQ Sims is editing his first novel, a work of speculative fiction that centers Queer characters, and he is mortified by the number of typos. Instagram *@t.q.sims*

Who am I to Keep You Down?

That strange hot summer my circle played the Fleetwood Mac album constantly. Half the crowd stepped out on each other. Was it correlation or real causation? Couples split from the fallout. No one local suffered like Lindsey Buckingham, who ripped fingertips playing pick-less on hit songs about his shortcomings.

Todd Mercer writes fiction and poetry in Grand Rapids, Michigan, and he loves this life.

Splashing Out

Self-conscious about an undiagnosed skin disease he's developed from somewhere while on his budget travels, Donald keeps covered up. But after one night of oppressive Thai heat and little sleep, he upgrades to the posh hotel with A/C and a pool. Cannonballing in, he thinks, *It's only French kids*.

Originally from Missouri, Sherry Morris writes prize-winning fiction from a farm in the Scottish Highlands where she pets cows, watches clouds, and dabbles in photography. *uksherka.com*

Rosary

Janie's weary mother sews ice-blue taffeta, dry-clicking her prayers. Downstairs the slick-haired hot-rod fiancé dances *Mama Told Me Not to Come* with eight of us down the line, "Gorgeous, guess I won't be sleepin' with you no more." He knows Janie is leaning against the door.

Anna Marie Laforest is a poet and cozy mystery novelist who can eat chocolate and listen to opera at the same time. *annamarielaforest.wixsite.com*

Virgilio

Handsome, sundrenched, meticulous attire he orchestrates the seaside café like a conductor, the menu his baton and the tourist musicians. A smile that never abates when inquired, "Who owned the house on the beach?" The sage reply, "Christopher Columbus!" and guests believe because he lulls them with pleasant notes.

Deb Obermanns is an avid traveler, lover of storytelling, and international school teacher.

When the Heart Stops Writing

I stopped writing and the nightmare returned. Back in college, I must pass English to graduate but can't find the classroom. No map. So, why not save my ancient heart by doing what I love doing? I tried but couldn't find a roadmap either to steer around my writer's block.

Marc Littman is a prolific writer of micro fiction as well as longer stories, novels, and plays.

El Callejero (aka Street Dog)

He had roamed the hard streets for a year. Squat legs and elongated torso, his front toes point outwards. Amiable by nature, he radiates pure joy. Until he encounters the unfamiliar. Dog trainers call it reactive. The air conditioner repairman empathized: "That's so sad. He's lost his trust in people."

Linda Doughty is a retired classical flute player who lives and writes in the Sonoran Desert, secure in the knowledge that saguaros are our friends. *lindadoughty.com*

Last Conversation

Your wide eyes seemed childlike on your emaciated face.

"Do you know what's happening?" I asked.

You nodded.

Unsure if you knew what I was asking, I continued, "Next time, don't refuse morphine."

I was practical until the end that I didn't know was the end. And you let me.

A special education teacher by day, Theresa Milstein writes middle grade, YA, and dabbles in poetry. *theresamilstein.blogspot.com*

The Knob

The knob of her bathroom door turned slowly. She'd gone in to change into something more comfortable. I held my breath. She came out wearing a burqa. "This is so much better," she said. "Now you won't be distracted, and we can get to know each other."

Michael Fryd, a retired scientist, writes fiction in Philadelphia.

Bloody Mary Says Hi

Stare into a mirror, flashlight under your chin. Classmates believe Bloody Mary appears. I want to be these girls, so I comply. My skin glows reddish, my breath shallow, haunted eyes gaze back. The mirror stretches for miles until Mary, many Marys, make their way forward and invite me in.

Joanne Nelson is the keeper of many unlabeled shoe boxes. She is the author of *This Is How We Leave* and the forthcoming, *My Neglected Gods* (2023). *wakeupthewriterwithin.com*

Her Reading Garden

She created the perfect morning escape. Pansies and violas, hostas, and peonies. She dug and planted for days. The final touch—a wicker chair and table. The next morning, with coffee and book in hand, she startled a deer for whom her reading garden had been the perfect breakfast.

Rita Riebel Mitchell writes tiny bits of fiction every day. She lives in the Pinelands of South Jersey with her favorite beta reader.

At Madam Olga's

Madam Olga stared into her crystal ball. Ralph waited ... Then more staring ... More waiting ...

Do you see anything, Madam Olga?

I'm looking ...

Any chance for success?

I'm looking ...

How about love? ... Or even a little money?

I'm looking, I'm looking ...

David Sydney is a physician from Newtown, PA.

Purple Glaze

Young peoples' eyes have taken to glazing over as boomers wax nostalgically about the wonders of the psychedelic sixties. Many in that age group have developed a disdain for the older generation. However, eye glazing and disdain by the young for the old is not exactly a new phenomenon.

Roy Dorman enjoys reading and writing speculative fiction and poetry.

Bridge

My last day in Budapest, I scoured the shops to find a gift for my sister. I found an elegant cameo pin with a profile that looked like her, aristocratic. Yesterday, I discovered the pin in my dresser, never gifted to her. Will I ever bridge the distance between us?

Robin Mayer Stein, of Hungarian descent, writes fiction and poetry about family matters from her perch in Massachusetts. *robinsteincreative.com*

Like Herding Cats

Some lined up immediately. Others dawdled, compliant but begrudging. Then, Worry hopped from foot to foot. Insecurity began to pace. Anxiety spun in rapid circles that would surely induce vomiting. Shame scurried, frenetically searching for a hiding place. Ms. Brain sighed. Ironic how chaos always erupted during meditation time.

Elizabeth Barton rearranges words for fun and profit while living in Chicago with her husband, two cats, and ample self-doubt. *lizardesque.wordpress.com*

Emergency Chair

My classroom has a new chair, molded plastic, Crayola blue. Masking tape marks the back left metal leg, which slides behind the door handle to jam the door shut with one quick twist. I practiced—it works—but I haven't shown students yet. No need to upset them, admin decreed.

Beth Manca teaches Latin to enthusiastic middle school students.

Hot Mom Life

Family vacation in Wildwood, two weeks after giving birth to my
    second child.
Sweltering heat and a nursing newborn is almost overwhelmingly
    claustrophobic.
"Aunt Mona, the pool is so refreshing. Come on in!"
Something tells me they wouldn't feel the same way once all my
    postpartum, leaking orifices submerge.

Mona Soliman is a high school English teacher and storyteller.

Regrets

The corsages, fancy gowns, tuxedos. The innocence that exudes
into the darkness of mistrust, a desire to blend in, cover the
past. "The night was perfect." He kisses her on the cheek.
Her smile and clear blue eyes try to hide smeared make-up.
She always wanted to say more.

Danielle Boska is an English teacher by day and a lover of sports, words, books,
life, my two boys, and husband by night. Facebook @danielle.elizabeth

Strange Planet

I'm on a strange planet. Sounds are louder, smells stronger. Sometimes the light is too bright. Even physical sensations can be too much. The people here are strange. They communicate in odd ways. I don't understand them, nor they me. I'm told I have a disorder. They call it autism.

Shea Ballard is a fantasy writer who lives in the Phoenix area. *sheaballard.com*

End of Sixth Grade

She got them at age ten.
Now they were twelve.
"That was your last test," she said.
"Don't we have a cumulative?" one asked.
She explained they'd do games and puzzles instead.
They murmured in unabashed enthusiasm to each other.
    She hoped they'd stay this sweet when they turned teen.

A special education teacher by day, Theresa Milstein writes middle grade, YA, and dabbles in poetry. *theresamilstein.blogspot.com*

No Letter G

Slate-blue eyes, platinum hair, an enduring smile Theo has his own language. Burrowing his delicate toddler hand into Downie's apron pocket while she bakes raisin buns. It's she who encompasses his heart and why "Downie"? Because Granny is a "G" word that limits his creativity, but not his love.

Deb Obermanns is an avid traveler, lover of storytelling, and international school teacher.

My 22-Square-Meter Parisian Studio

Six hours post-sex with a hunky American tourist, I crouch on my toilet seat and reach for the slippery, circular dome in the hinterlands of my vagina as every organ cinches, my diaphragm trapped in space, surely punishment for sleeping with a stranger. Call it karma?

Jen Lang is a California transplant in Tel Aviv, whose prize-winning essays appear in various journals and whose memoir *Places We Left Behind*, will be published by Vine Leaves Press, 2023. Facebook @israelwritersstudio

Our Eyes Met

Our eyes met. Love at first sight. We married in Tahiti and then settled in an old farmhouse with several chickens and cats, and we adopted two children,. Growing old was sweet, and our love never faded.

"That'll be $35.00, please."

I swiped my debit card and left the store.

Michael Yoder is a published writer living in Victoria BC Canada. His work includes short stories and novellas.

Wedding Plans

Boadicea, in designer jump suit, standing at the helm. Her cape in full flow on super woman shoulders, all pride and pout, huntress, conquering all. The superlative elegance of the salon nods to its up and coming, elite. Final fitting done, the question was, how to accessorize? Bling and fizz, she decides, in superlative, automatic gesture.

Jenny Dunbar continues to make ceramics and haikus in these strange times.

Woolf at the Door

Dottie grew up slapped and scolded, her lips forming a permanent O. She asked me for a list of woman-centered novels, and I happily typed up my favs. A week later she had a black eye; her husband had found the list. She said she would not blame me.

Anna Marie Laforest is a poet and cozy mystery novelist who can eat chocolate and listen to opera at the same time. *annamarielaforest.wixsite.com/stories*

The Stunt

Ralph conceived of his greatest stunt yet. Blindfolded, holding a bowl containing five goldfish in one hand, he would juggle five ping-pong paddles in the other. He already had a blindfold and four paddles. All he had to do was learn to juggle and get five fish and a paddle.

David Sydney is a physician from Newtown, PA.

Him & Me

The world was too small for the both of us. So I let the world go—let it spin away from me and into the hands of the monsters. Inside me is space. Blackness. Stars. The future. Rage. A royal flush. Checkmate. Inside me is a chair. Sit down. Listen.

A.S. King is an award-winning author, a teacher, and she is building an invisible house out of poetry. *as-king.com*

Vine Leaves Press

Enjoyed this book?

Go to *vineleavespress.com* to find more.

Subscribe to our newsletter: